Bubbles

Book 2: Danger at Christmas

Dale J. Moore

Published by Northern Amusements, Inc., LaSalle, Ontario.

This is a work of fiction. All of the characters, organizations, and events portrayed in this novel are either products of the author's imagination or are used fictitiously.

Bubbles Book 2: Danger at Christmas / Dale J. Moore - 1st Edition Trade Paperback

ISBN 978-0-9868 534-5-6

This book and others by Northern Amusements are available in electronic format.

ISBN 978-0-9868 534-6-3

Cover by Dale J. Moore
Edited by Maureen P. Moore
Author photo by Linda Moore
Printed and bound in the United States and/or Canada.

Dedications

To Linda, Justin, and Melissa, for their inspiration and continued support. Humour is the backbone of great storytelling and strong families.

Table of Contents

0   Getting Ready

Sitting in his bathtub, playing with a mound of bubbles that he referred to by name, Benjay Marshall closed his eyes to remember. Several months and a birthday had passed since he'd encountered the Bubbles. For an eight-year-old boy, it seemed like forever since he'd seen his real-life Bubble friend, Peepers. Their adventure with her Bubble family and his family seemed more like a bedtime story his mother had read to him than something he had lived. If his sister, Lindsay, didn't frequently remind him, he'd think the whole thing was created in his imagination in the tub with the bubbles he played with now. A real live Bubble that talked, flew, could go invisible, and zip through walls like thin air – that was beyond his young imagination.

"Benjay," his mother called from outside the bathroom. "Time to get out. Do you need any help?"

"Okay, Mom," he called back. "I'll let you know if I need any help." He knew she'd wait for him to emerge, still worried he'd slip getting out or while putting on his repaired prosthetic leg, Prosty. He successfully maneuvered out of the tub. Momentarily he looked at the toilet seat for his pajamas before remembering it was early evening. He needed to put on clothes.

"Are you okay in there, Benjay?"

"Yes, Mom." He paused. "Maybe you can help me with these buttons?"

His mother entered. Kneeling, she smiled looking at her son's attempt that left gaps and humps on the front of his shirt. "Let me fix it."

"Why did I have to have my bath so early tonight?"

"Tonight is the Christmas party at my work."

Paul State Bank hosted an annual Christmas party. The Marshalls hadn't attended in a couple of years due to Benjay's health issues. He could tell she was excited about it. Or maybe she was nervous. He had trouble telling those two apart sometimes.

"I could have had my bath when I got home, before bed like I always do."

"Your father and I thought you'd be too tired. We'll be out late. You'll likely fall asleep on the car ride home."

Benjay protested, standing as tall as he was able. "I'm not a kid anymore. I'm eight years old now."

His mother tried hiding a laugh, or perhaps a tear? "Lindsay had her shower earlier for the same reason, and she's older than you. She didn't complain."

"But ..." he started, though he really didn't know what he would say in his defence. It might have had something to do with her being a girl – his go-to argument when he didn't want to do something his sister had to do.

"Benjay," she cut him off. "You just have to trust that your mom and dad know what's best for you, understand?"

Benjay looked down, nodding. "Sorry, Mom."

"Apology accepted." She finished tucking in his shirt. Leaning back, she looked him up and down. "Did you forget to wash your face again?"

"Maybe…"

She finished roughing up his face with a soapy washcloth. "There!" she exclaimed. "Handsome, just like your father."

Benjay grinned ear to ear.

Downstairs in the living room, Benjay's father sat reading a book. Lindsay paced anxiously.

"There you are. Finally!" she exclaimed at the sight of her brother navigating down the stairs using the railings that her father had installed on both sides of the stairs. She knew better than to offer him help, though she really wanted to speed him up and get on their way. Her friend's mother worked at the same bank, but the local branch, not the main office. The two twelve-year-olds planned to hang out together. The party invite posted on the fridge with an angel-shaped magnet mentioned tree decorating, gingerbread house making, shortbread cookie decorating, face painting, and holiday-themed games with prizes.

"I checked the forecast," Mr. Marshall said to his wife. "Only light white stuff until tomorrow afternoon. Should be a good drive downtown."

In the car, Benjay stared out the window as they drove, looking at the few inches of snow on the ground he'd played in all day. With Lindsay's help, they made a couple of ginormous snowmen at least her height on the front lawn. He didn't realize her strength, able to lift those big snowballs on top of each other. They'd gotten some burnt chocolate chip cookies from Grandma Marshall the day before, which Benjay flipped over to use for black eyes on the snowmen. A big crow had landed on one of the snowmen, pecking away at the cookie. It flew away squawking, unable to chip off a piece with its sharp beak. The kids fell on the snow laughing. At least what remained of the snow. They'd rolled so many snowballs that most of the grass showed again.

"Mom?" Benjay called up to the front seat.

"Yes, dear?"

"Why do you work at the Paul State Bank downtown and not the one where we live? Where is Paul state? I don't remember seeing it on a map. Is it near Missippipi?"

Lindsay snorted a laugh.

His mother replied. "It's Mississippi. There is no state named Paul. It's just a state bank, named after the founder, Mr. Jacob Paul. The one near us is a small branch office. I work downtown at the main branch because that's where they do the type of work that I do."

"Oh," Benjay responded, tentatively.

"She manages large commercial accounts, like big stores and factories," Lindsay chimed, recalling what she'd learned at parent-child day. "Right, Mom?"

Her mother grinned. "That's right, dear."

"Commercials? Did you manage the commercial for Super Jet Flying Alien action figures?" Benjay gleefully asked.

Benjay's dad laughed. "Not those type of commercials, kiddo."

Satisfied with that reply, Benjay asked, "How old is the bank? It looks like it's even older than Grandpa, and he must be a hundred years old."

Mrs. Marshall smirked at her husband. "You are correct, it's older than that. Did you know that the first bank at that location was built about two hundred years ago?"

"Wow." Benjay's eyes lit up, imaging cowboys pulling up on their horses to his mother's bank.

"They rebuilt it in the early 1930's. It's beautiful inside, with the marble floors, mahogany woodwork, and a twenty metre ceiling. It feels like working in a castle or palace." She laughed to herself. "Especially when it gets really cold outside."

"Why's that?" Lindsay asked.

"It's hard to heat a big, cavernous space like that. Hot air rises, so the cold air tends to stay down where we work. Mr. Paul's office on the balcony feels much warmer. The large revolving doors at the front cut down on some of the warm air escaping and cold outside air getting in."

"Alright, we're here," Mr. Marshall called out. "Just need to park."

1   Seer

On her way to school with the other children in her family, Peepers glanced up. The Globe in the sky they called home had transparent sections for viewing outside, and letting natural light in. Since school occurred overnight for Bubbles, she spotted the full moon in all its radiant glory. A full moon meant the time had come to ask again. She had asked every full moon following her trip to the surface where she met the bald, machine-boy Benjay. On an informal surface ban by the Elders, her mother had given Fret instructions to hold off taking Peepers to the surface until further notice. Being winter, she couldn't explore the ponds and streams she loved anyway. The waters began to freeze over. Most of her little bug friends had hibernated. Still, she missed seeing the human boy. He was a wondrous curiosity to her.

13

Moving close to her oldest brother, Peepers asked, "Fret?" She continued to stare at the glowing moon.

Fret looked at his younger sister, seeing her staring up at the moon. He sighed, then replied. "Yes, Peepers. What can I help you with?" He thought he knew the question but thought it a day early.

"I was just wondering if I might be allowed to make a trip to the surface soon?"

"I will talk to Mom tomorrow morning. I don't think she will let you go just yet."

"Okay, thanks for asking Mom!" Peepers tried to sound bubbly and hopeful. Inside she knew the chances were not good. Last full moon, her mom had told Fret 'likely a few more full moons.' While only one had passed, she wanted to see if her mom had changed her mind. Her mom had already told her not to come directly to her for that question, but to ask Fret. That resulted from Peepers asking her mom every few days during the first full moon after her trip.

Arriving at school, Peepers's family was greeted with the unexpected news of an assembly. Sometimes assemblies were held by specific classes that had a play or songs to share with the whole school. Those were okay, but Peepers enjoyed the ones where they had guest speakers. She liked the guest speakers that shared fascinating stories of the history of the Bubbles. Her favourite speakers were ones that shared stories of the surface. The students buzzed with excitement in the assembly hall, knowing no student led activities were scheduled. Murmurs filled the air about the guest speaker and their topic.

"Welcome, students," Principal Wisdom announced, the guessing fading away. "We have a special guest who has travelled a long way to visit the Bulle clan today. Our guest comes from the Bolha clan."

The students chattered with excitement. Likely none of them had met a Bolha clan member.

"She travelled here on Elder business. She volunteered to share her special abilities with us. Nobody in our clan has her unique skill. Her name is Seer. She can see into a person's future."

The crowd noise exploded.

"Please," Wisdom continued, motioning for quiet. "She will tell you that she is not always correct. Outside circumstances can change the future. I know from a session she held with the Elders yesterday, she can provide incredible insight. Please give a warm welcome to our guest, Seer."

The crowd responded with loud applause.

"Thank you," Seer said. She made an arm, putting it up above her eyes. "I see all of you will go home tonight and do your homework and chores."

The crowd groaned.

"Just joking. That's not what I do, but I'm sure you'll all do your best to keep up with your studies. For today, we will randomly draw two students' names. We'll bring one up at a time. I'll work with them to predict their future. What you will hear, I extract from thoughts in the victim's mind – oh, did I say victim," she laughed. "I meant helper. If you think about your mother, my prediction will likely focus on something between you and your mother. Got it? Good. Principal Wisdom, if you would be kind enough to bring me the container with the students' names."

The principal rolled out a small, spinning drum that the school had used before to draw door prizes at special events. The students could see the tiles with their names floating around inside. Seer opened the lid and reached inside. The students could see her form a scoop at the end of her arm. A tile floated into it. She pulled out her arm to read the name.

"Peepers? Am I reading that right, Wisdom?"

The principal looked at the tile, nodding.

Peepers shot out from the crowd to the stage. She trembled with excitement.

"A little nervous, are you?" asked Seer, smiling.

All Peepers could do was shake yes.

"Okay, look into my eyes. Relax. You may feel a little sleepy, but this isn't hypnosis. You're just going into a meditative state of sorts."

Peepers stared into Seer's peaceful eyes, feeling a calm come over her body.

"Good," Seer told her. "I'm going to close my eyes now to peer into your thoughts. You can keep your eyes open or close them. Your choice."

Peepers slowly closed her eyes.

"I'm getting some images," Seer said, starting her task. "I see a boy. A human boy. He's different though. He's got a mechanical leg."

The crowd gasped. Peepers opened her eyes.

"Just relax, dear," Seer told her. "I see this boy. It's snowing outside. He's in a big human building. I see someone – I think it's his mother – no wait, smaller, must be a sister. Now I see his mother. Oh dear! He's in trouble. Some bad people have trapped him. He's in trouble. He needs help!"

Seer's eyes opened, staring at Peepers. "Does any of that make sense, my dear? It's a very unusual reading of the future, to be sure."

Peepers went back to trembling. Her voice quivered,

"Yes, …. Benjay's in trouble."

2 The Holiday Party

Benjay had visited the downtown bank a few years ago, at least
according to his mom. He didn't remember it at all. Walking
across the street from the parking lot, Benjay looked at the
majestic building.

"Wow! That doesn't look anything like a bank. It looks
like a museum."

"In some ways, it is a museum, with the old architecture
and design," his mother replied. "Now, you remember what we
talked about, Benjay?"

He nodded. "I don't leave your side, unless it's with
Dad, or holding Lindsay's hand."

"And?"

"And don't eat so much candy that I'm heaving chunks tomorrow."

"Benjay Marshall! Where did you learn such a phrase?"

Benjay glanced at Lindsay, who quickly shook her head. "Uh, I think I heard it on SpongeBob."

Lindsay winked at her brother for covering for her.

"Well, please don't repeat that tonight, okay?"

Benjay nodded, looking up at the bank's revolving front door. "That door is as tall as our house!"

"It just looks that way, buddy," his father replied. "But it is heavy. I don't think you can spin that one around by yourself."

Entering the door, Benjay pushed mightily, the door barely moving. Suddenly, the large door sprung forward, causing him to lose his balance and fall. Lindsay, who'd pushed the door above him, stumbled over him, bouncing her shoulder off the glass door, and falling through the opening onto the bank floor. She looked back to see Benjay sprawled in the doorway. Her mother had a stern, unhappy look, standing in the turnstile opening behind where Benjay lay. Her father suppressed a laugh, seeing both kids looked unharmed. Benjay rolled to his side, checked Prosty remained in place, then got up, unaware what had happened.

The security guard approached Benjay entering the bank. "Are you okay, son?"

Benjay looked up. "I'm fine, sir. Thank you."

The guard retreated to his post by the door.

"Sorry, Lindsay," Benjay apologized. "Guess I pushed too hard."

"No, little bro." She leaned down to look in his eyes. "My bad. I got tired of you not budging the door and gave it a giant push. Are you okay?"

"Yep."

"Good." She smacked him on his bald head. The sound echoed in the large open space.

"Cool," Benjay said. "Do it again!"

"No, you don't!" Their mother quietly snapped at them. "Everybody is already looking at you two."

The kids looked around. It was true. A lot of eyes looked in their direction. With people turning away after the initial excitement, the Marshall kids looked around the inside of the building. The glossy floor showcased a large rectangular black outer border. Fancy tiles with a diamond-like design covered the rest of the floor. One side of the bank looked like the banks Benjay had seen – with a row of teller counters where people could make deposits and withdrawals. The other side had a row of offices, with beautiful wooden doors with embossed glass windows that you couldn't see through. Above the row of offices was another single, large office. A stairway led there from the front of the building, with a rope strewn across it to prevent access tonight. A sad looking undecorated Christmas tree stood next to the staircase. Benjay's gaze drifted up to the high ceiling.

Looking down again, Benjay spotted something between the shoulders of his mother and father.

"No way!" he declared. He pushed between his parents. "That must be the biggest Christmas tree I've ever seen!" Near

24

the back of the bank stood a lit, fully decorated towering tree. The star at the top seemed to scrape the ceiling.

"I'm glad we don't have to decorate that one!" Lindsay laughed. Around the bank, ready for trimming, stood a half-dozen much smaller trees like the one near the doorway. They each stood about three metres. Lights and various tree toppers were in place, unlit, waiting for decorations.

"And look, Mom!" Benjay spotted the setup in front of the large tree. A large red chair with gold trim, oversized bags of presents, and a queue. "You didn't tell me about Santa coming here tonight! I want to see him first!"

A female elf approached them. "One to see Santa today?"

Mrs. Marshall looked at Lindsay, who shook her head no. She shot her mom a 'really?' look.

"Yes, one please."

The elf held out a small gift bag to Benjay. "Pick out a number."

Benjay reached, swirling the numbers around. He pulled out number twenty-four.

The elf gave instructions. "We elves will call kids up twelve at a time to get in line for Santa. We call it the 'twelve kids of Christmas'," she laughed to herself. "You, young man, are in the second group we call."

Benjay frowned.

"Don't be sad," the elf replied. "There are other activities and goodies to enjoy before your turn, okay? And some of the numbers may not get picked by kids, making it quicker."

Benjay nodded, smiling.

Her mother looked at the invitation for agenda details. "Santa starts later. Let's get something to drink. My boss makes a toast in fifteen minutes. No activities until after the toast."

"Can I go find Marcia?" Lindsay asked, bouncing up and down excitedly.

"Well, I'm not sure …" her mother started to say.

Her father put a reassuring hand on her mother's arm. "Yes, give me your coat, then place these canned goods in the donation box over there." He motioned toward it. "Meet us over there by the beverage stand in ten minutes. We're going to put the toys for the needy under the tree." He looked at his daughter and pointed at his watch. "Ten minutes, no more."

"Yes, sir!" she pointed at her fitness watch, then saluted. She started to run off, stopping with a sheepish grin to take off her coat. She sat the canned goods on the floor, removed her coat, and handed it to him. "Sorry," she hurriedly said, then rushed off to find her friend, leaving the canned goods on the floor.

Mrs. Marshall shook her head, picked up the canned goods, and walked the few short steps to place them in the donation box. Before placing the toys under the tree, Mr. Marshall and Benjay visited her office to hang their coats and lock up her purse.

"Let me go freshen up while you drop off the donated gifts," Sonya Marshall said to her husband.

"Sure, hon. We'll meet you at the beverage station." He gave her a peck on the cheek. "Okay, buddy. Let's get these gifts dropped off before you open the packages and start playing with them."

The Marshall family had brought a bright yellow plastic dump truck and matching excavator. Benjay had been dying to play with them from the moment he helped his mom pick them out at the store a couple of weeks ago. He carried the dump truck, his father the excavator. Benjay let out a full open-mouthed 'wow' as the tree grew taller and taller looking as they moved closer. A couple of women in elf outfits collected the gifts, placing them on tables by the tree. Benjay looked around. Already on the tables were drones, handheld video games, board games, remote control cars, Super Jet Flying Alien action figures, building block sets, baseball gloves, mini hockey sets, art sets, and lots of other cool stuff. He also spotted some yucky girl stuff like dress up dolls and makeup kits.

"Those needy kids are sure lucky," Benjay said, looking at his dad. His father gave him the 'look.' "Oh, I don't mean they are lucky to be needy … I mean lucky that all these people help give them something for Christmas."

"Yes, Benjay. We donate every Christmas, and at other times throughout the year. Your mother was very poor at your age. Did you know that?"

"No, I didn't."

"Grandma and Grandpa both worked two jobs to improve their way of life, and to pay for your mother's university tuition."

"No wonder they always look tired and take naps in the afternoon."

"No wonder," he replied, laughing out loud.

3   Mr. Paul

Sipping on a hot chocolate, waiting by an undecorated tree next to the beverage stand, Mr. Marshall checked his watch. Right on time, Lindsay and her friend Marcia arrived, giggling about something.

"What's so funny?" Benjay asked.

"That's for me to know and you to find out," Lindsay replied, still giggling.

"It can't be important then," Benjay replied, though deep inside he died to know.

"If you must know … see that man over there?" She tried to point, without pointing. "That shorter man with the plaid shirt. Do you see him?"

"Yep, what about him?"

"He left his shirt untucked in the back, hanging out over his butt."

"What's so funny about that?"

"Never mind, then. We thought he looked funny."

Mrs. Marshall looked at her daughter. "You know it's not right to make fun of other people."

"Yes, mom," Lindsay replied, suppressing her giggle.

"That's Mr. Wilson. He works with me." She lowered her voice, leaning over to whisper, "His shirt is always untucked like that. He doesn't seem to care that he looks weird."

Lindsay smiled, trying to keep a straight face.

"My boss, Mr. Paul, will speak any minute now," Mrs. Marshall said, straightening up.

"Is he related to that man Jacob Paul who founded the bank?"

"Yes, dear. His great, great, great, great grandfather, or something like that."

"When do we get to see Santa and play games?" interrupted Benjay.

"After his speech, likely." Benjay's mother replied. "Oh, here comes Paul now."

"I thought you said it was Mr. Paul," Benjay asked.

"It is, dear."

"Then why did you call him Paul, and not Mr. Paul?"

"I call my co-workers by their first names, even my boss."

"Wait," Lindsay said, dramatically holding up her hand. "Your boss's name is Paul Paul?"

"Yes," her mother replied. "Paul Paul, the fourth, to be precise."

"No way! That's too funny," Lindsay replied, loud enough that the people around her stared. "Sorry," she said, covering her mouth. "Is his son Paul Paul the fifth?"

"I believe he is."

"I think they should have stuck with Jacob."

Her mother smiled. "Now hush; there's Mr. Paul now."

The crowd applauded the man walking to the microphone placed in front of Santa's throne.

The man waited for the clapping to fade. "Welcome, everyone. Thank you very much for attending tonight's holiday party." The tall, skinny man looked fragile, like you could snap his arms like twigs. Premature grey had completely turned his hair white many years ago, what remained. He had a noticeable hunch, making his left shoulder hang lower. The hunch seemed to drag his face down too, scrunched and a bit contorted. His left eye barely cracked open. "I am thrilled to see such an abundant and stupendous turnout. I am overwhelmed by the generosity of the magnanimous gesture you've displayed with your charitable donations of canned goods and toys for those in peril in our great community."

Whispering to his dad, Benjay said. "He sure says a lot of big words."

"Undoubtedly," he replied.

Mr. Paul continued. "Let's have a round of applause for our organizing committee, led by Mrs. Peters." He pointed an open hand in the direction of a petite blond woman in the front. She waved her hand up high. He paused for a moment. "Thank you all. You young kids may have noticed a large red velvet chair behind me. Santa will arrive in," he checked his watch, "about thirty minutes." He paused again for the excited buzz to die down. "Until then, and all night, there are game and activity stations set up around the bank for you all to enjoy … and maybe win a prize or two!" Some kids yipped with excitement. "And don't forget to visit the food and beverage areas. Thanks again everyone. Have a great evening!"

"I volunteered to help with the food setup for a few minutes, then I'll meet up with you," Mrs. Marshall told her group.

"Well, kids. What do you want to do first?" Mr. Marshall asked. "And don't say Santa, Benjay. They'll call your number when it's your turn."

Benjay yelled out 'Santa Bag Toss.'

Lindsay said, "Whack a Grinch.'

"Okay, we'll start with 'Santa Bag Toss,' since it is closest, then move on to 'Whack a Grinch'".

A couple kids waited in front of them when they arrived at the 'Santa Bag Toss.' The game had an elf helping explain the rules, even though a rules sign stood next to the throwing line. Each contestant got three Santa bags – bean bags covered in a small Santa-style bag. If a player got one in the hole, they got their choice of prizes. If they landed on the board, the elf picked their prize.

"Are we ready to start?" The elf said to those in line.

"Yes!" they called out.

The elf picked up the bags from the board. Standing up she noticed a guest. "Look, Mr. Paul has stopped by to cheer you on."

The boss clapped his hands. "Good luck, kids."

Benjay got a closer look at his mother's boss. He looked kind of scary. He couldn't decide if Mr. Paul looked mean, too. The way the man hunched over frightened him a bit. He remembered what his mother said about not judging a book by its cover. His mother said the man was nice. That was good enough for Benjay.

The first boy, about ten years old, missed on his first two throws. His final one landed on the board. The elf looked at him, reached into her bag, pulling out a Hot Wheels car. The kid grinned, said thanks, and moved to the side to let his much younger sister throw. The young girl missed all three tries, landing three or four feet short on each toss. The girl pouted.

"Don't worry, sweetie," the elf smiled. "You tried your best." Reaching into her bag, she pulled out a small doll.

The girl turned her frown upside down, leaving happy.

Marcia went next, and landing one on the board, received a small pack of temporary Christmas tattoos.

"Let me show you how it's done, little bro," Lindsay told Benjay, confidently stepping up to the line. Her first bag sailed through the air, hit the board, slid barely past the hole, and dropped off the back. Benjay and Marcia each let out an 'oooh.' Her next toss spun through the air, passing right through the hole.

"Woohoo," yelled Marcia, Lindsay jumping up and down.

Lindsay looked through the prizes available. She really liked a light up Christmas bracelet, holding it up to admire it for a few seconds. Instead, she picked the same prize as Marcia.

Benjay stepped to the line. His first toss landed about five feet short of the board. He grabbed the second bag, tossing it harder, yet still landing just short of the board. Determined, he grabbed the third bag, throwing it as hard as he could – overhand. Benjay lost his balance releasing the bag. The bag sailed past the board, hitting Mr. Paul – right in the private area. The already hunching man buckled over further for a moment, then slowly stood up.

"I'm alright," the man replied with a forced grin, raising his hand, gasping for air.

Mr. Marshall walked over to apologize and see if the man was really okay.

Benjay blushed and started to walk away.

"Wait," the elf called out. "You still get a prize." She reached into her bag, tossing him a small elf doll.

"Thanks," Benjay smiled.

"He'll be fine," Benjay's dad told them as he returned. "He's more embarrassed than hurt."

"I'm sorry, dad. I lost my balance."

His dad rubbed the boy's bald head. "No problem, son. At least your mother didn't see it."

They walked to the next game, getting in line. Two 'Whack a Grinch' games stood side by side. Like the Santa Bag Toss, if you reached a certain score, you got to pick your prize. Otherwise, the elf did. They watched the two players pound away, trying to hit the Grinch while not hitting any Whoville characters. Two pairs waited ahead of Lindsay and Marcia.

Mr. Paul came up behind them, looking fully recovered from the earlier incident. He had a young girl with him.

"We're so sorry about … before," Mr. Marshall told him.

"No problem," Mr. Paul replied. "My granddaughter here wants to give this one a try." She looked about Benjay's age.

"Attention," began an announcement, "Santa will arrive soon! Can we have children with numbers one to twelve get in line please – with their parents, of course."

"Cool," Benjay said, bouncing around to spot the big guy's entrance.

The next pair in line began their turns. As they finished, the next announcement came.

"He's here, everyone! Let's greet Santa and his elves with a big round of applause."

The kids all yelled out, including Benjay. He felt nervous about his turn with Santa.

The game waiting line nudged one pair closer. The kids tried to see what kind of prizes waited for winning at this game. They spotted some of the same prizes used for the last game, with a few ones they hadn't seen. Lindsay and Marcia moved up to take their turn, both pounding on the board with vigor. When the game stopped, Marcia had barely beaten Lindsay, both beating the score to pick their own prize. This time, they grabbed the lighted bracelet Lindsay had admired earlier.

"I thought I was going to win. Did your hammer feel weird near the end?" Lindsay asked.

"No, what do you mean?" Marcia responded.

"Like it was wobbly, or something."

Marcia shook her head.

Benjay moved up to take Lindsay's spot. Mr. Paul's granddaughter lined up beside him.

"Ready?" The elf asked. The kids nodded. "Go."

The two eight-year-olds pounded away at the game, smashing anything that moved, Grinch or not. Not really the object of the game but having a blast. Benjay felt his hammer getting wobblier the more he hit it. He swung down on a Grinch, pulling the mallet back quickly. The head of the hammer flew off the handle, launching backward. Mr. Marshall leaned hard to the side to avoid the flying object; it hit Mr. Paul square in the chest.

He gasped and hunched over. Benjay stood in shock, looking at the man.

"Grandpa – are you okay?" The girl rushed to the side of her bent-over grandfather.

Gasping, he replied, "Quite so, my dear." Catching his breath, he straightened up. "I think Grandpa's had enough games for tonight. Get your prize and let's find your mother."

"Again, we're so sorry, Mr. Paul," said a concerned Mr. Marshall.

"An accident. Just bad luck where I was standing." He looked over at the elf. "I'm sure our friendly elf will check the mallets between games from now on." She nodded back, surprised at what had happened, and anxious to avoid a repeat.

Mr. Marshall looked at his kids. "Benjay, this wasn't your fault, okay?"

Benjay nodded, still embarrassed.

"I want to catch up with your mother," his father said. "I'm sure she'll want to reintroduce me to some of her coworkers. How about you kids head over to the gingerbread station? Something that doesn't involve throwing or hammering might be a good change of pace. Sound good?"

They nodded yes.

"Lindsay," he added. "Keep Benjay at your side. When you're done with your gingerbread house, come find us, okay?"

4   Bad Feeling

The night at school dragged on for Peepers. The future prediction

for the other student had tamed in comparison to Peepers's

reading by Seer. She worried about the Benjay reading all night,

unable to concentrate in her classes. It also felt like everyone

stared at her. At the end of the day, she never felt happier to see

her brothers and sisters. They comforted her, telling her not to

worry about her human friend Benjay. After all, they said, the

seer wasn't always right. Sometimes she misinterpreted images

that came to her mind. She thanked each of them for their

support, not conveying what she really thought. She'd wait to get

Fret alone at home – after chores.

"Fret, I'm worried sick about Benjay. Assuming Seer is

correct, he and his family are in danger."

"We don't know that for sure."

"Yes, we do. Didn't you see the look on Seer's face when she finished the reading? She felt afraid for Benjay. Honestly scared. I could tell."

"It likely surprised her, not knowing your recent experience with humans."

"Maybe, but it looked like more than that, big brother." She paused. "I need to go see for myself if Benjay is in trouble."

"Mother will be home shortly. I will talk to her as soon as she arrives. Okay? I understand your concern, but Bubbles do not go around rescuing humans. There are thousands of them in danger every day. We can't interfere like that."

Peepers frowned.

"Maybe what Seer saw today will change Mom's mind. I will ask if she heard. That's the best I can do."

Peepers cracked a small smile. "Thanks, Fret."

An hour later, their mother, Hope, arrived home. She met with the other Globe Elders every night to discuss business.

The Elders were chosen to lead their clan. She greeted and hugged each of the children. Looking around she smiled. "I see you've all done your chores! That makes me very happy." She addressed them as a group. "We Elders heard something exciting happened today in assembly."

Before Peepers could say anything, Jet blurted out, "It was amazing." She flew a quick circle around everyone. "Peepers's human friend is in danger."

The children's chatter rose to a deafening level. Their mother motioned for quiet.

"I see you are all excited about it. Fret is the oldest. Let me talk to him about it in private for a minute, then he will come back to tell you what the Elders had to say."

The children excitedly nodded in agreement. Peepers could barely contain her excitement. Maybe it was anxiety? Their mother led Fret to another room.

Once alone, she spoke.

"Seer gave the Elders a briefing of her reading with Peepers."

47

"It was pretty amazing, all the things she knew about Benjay," Fret told her.

"Not really, we possess a technique to probe other's thoughts that many Elders can perform. We rarely use the method, due to privacy concerns."

"I didn't know that."

"And you cannot repeat that. Do you understand?"

He nodded.

"Good. Her amazing skill is seeing glimpses of the future. She told us about Benjay being in danger. That is the immediate issue. I'm sure your sister Peepers is beside herself with worry."

"That, Mom, is an understatement," he smiled. "She asked me last night about going to see Benjay – before the meeting with the Seer."

"Interesting – coincidence, you think?"

"At first, I thought so. You know I've relayed her requests regularly to you. She asks me every full moon to go visit. But she asked me today – and the moon is not quite full.

Maybe she sensed something. She seems connected to that boy, somehow."

"I agree. That connection seems evident. However, the most interesting part of Seer's vision is what she *did not* say out loud to the assembly."

"She held something back?"

"Seer can, on occasion, see further out than a few days during a reading. She says it's very rare. It startles her whenever it happens."

"That would explain the look on her face. Peepers thought Seer felt scared for Benjay's safety."

"She is not wrong. Seer expressed sincere concern over the boy's well-being. Just not for the same reasons." She paused to compose herself. "What I'm telling you, you can never – and I mean never – tell anyone, especially your sister. You need to take the vow of silence on this issue."

Fret looked startled. He knew whatever he would hear next must be extremely sensitive. He made a couple of arms, making back and forth sweeping motions over his head. "I vow secrecy to what is about to be said."

"I'm glad you remembered the vow and movement," his mother smiled. "It may be the only time you ever use it, unless of course you get voted an Elder later in life." She paused again, moving close to whisper. "Seer only saw a few flashes beyond the next few days. From what she could make out, Benjay and the Bulle clan are connected. He is important to the future of the clan, possibly all Bubbles. It is vital that he stay safe."

"Wow," Fret whispered back, pressing his arms against his face.

"I couldn't have said it better. We Elders were stunned also."

"What does it mean, he's important to the Bulle clan?"

"Seer doesn't know. She had trouble interpreting the images. She said there was no mistake it was Benjay."

"That's kind of vague. Is she sure? She said that other factors can change what really happens."

"That's precisely her point. If something happens to Benjay, how does it impact the Bulle clan?"

"Oh, I see now," Fret replied.

"Here's where you get involved."

"Me?"

"Yes. The Elders want you to lead a reconnaissance mission to monitor Benjay's activity for a few days. They think you are ready to lead an off-Globe mission. Monitor only. No interaction unless necessary to save his life. The next part will sound cruel."

"What?"

"Do not intervene if Benjay is safe but someone in his family faces danger. For all we know, Benjay may be meant to live out his life without a parent. Sometimes tragedy makes people stronger, for example."

"That is cruel." He paused, thinking of his deceased father and the impact. "But I understand and will comply."

"Good. That may not be the hardest part of the mission." She broke her serious face, smiling at her son. "You have to take Peepers with you."

Fret laughed. "A challenge, for sure. At least it's not Jet. I can't keep up with her."

"Another Bubble will accompany you. Click. Do you know him?"

"Not really. I think he graduated a few years ago, didn't he?"

"That's correct. He's going to mentor you. He's your senior but will report to you to evaluate your decision making ability. He'll only take lead if necessary."

"Is Click the one that can take images with his mind, then project them in the air?"

"That's one skill. He can do other amazing things."

Fret nodded. "I'm not sure how he'll be able to help rescue Benjay."

Hope grinned. "It's the 'other amazing things' that may come in handy. Besides, he has a second mission. We're hoping

he can bring back images to share of the humans' Christmas
holiday. That will bring Christmas cheer to all Bulles."

"That would be nice," he replied. "And thanks for your
faith in me, Mom. I won't let you down."

5 Mingling

Randall Marshall caught up to his wife Sonya mingling after she completed her volunteer effort. She stood with a couple near the teller stations closest to the front of the bank.

"There you are, dear," she said to him on arrival.

"Just sent the kids to the gingerbread house station."

"Everything okay?"

"I'll tell you later. Let's just say Mr. Paul won't go near any more of their activities."

She gave him a funny look. She shrugged it off for now. "Dear, this is Joanelle Peters and Ramon Guapa."

"Nice to meet you." Randall looked them over. She pushed five feet tall, in her heels. Very pretty and petite, though her smile seemed a little forced. She likely clung to her forties.

Ramon looked in his mid-twenties – much younger than the two women. Standing about six-two, with square shoulders and a strong build, he attracted many looks from passersby. Randall spotted her wedding ring. "Fourteen years for us. How long have you two been together?"

Ramon blushed.

Joanelle put her hand up to her chest in shock. "We certainly are not a couple. I must be five or six years older than Ramon." She raised her chin in a look of superiority. "My husband travels overseas for work much of the year."

It was Randall's turn to blush. "Oh, my mistake."

"Joanelle is an executive commercial account manager, like me," his wife informed him. "Her office is beside mine. Ramon is a senior financial analyst who's worked at the bank about a year, maybe. Joanelle – how long have you been with Paul State?"

"Too long, some days," she laughed. "Let's just say I have seniority over everyone at the bank, except Paul."

"Joanelle has a large home in Riverview Estates," Sonya noted to her husband.

"It's not much, really. About eight thousand square feet, plus a two thousand foot guest house. Not to forget my husband's six-car garage, for his toys."

"Not much," Randall whispered to his wife.

"Must be a lot of upkeep," Ramon stated.

"We had people," Joanelle replied. "We sold the place a few weeks ago. We're moving out just before Christmas."

"Congratulations, Joanelle," Sonya said. "Where are you moving to?"

"Peter and I must look when he returns. I simply can't decide on my own. I've got a condo at Wiltshire Towers. We are shoving our stuff in storage for now."

"I thought your husband's name was Michael?" Ramon asked.

"What did I say?"

"Peter"

"Oh, I likely said Peters – sometimes I call him that."

Sonya glanced at Randall after the odd reply.

"What about you, Ramon? Where do you call home?"

"I've got an apartment a few blocks from here. I like the downtown vibe. You know, the small cafes, ethnic restaurants, quaint stores. Nothing beats skipping the daily drive and walking to work. Don't even have a car. Not sure I'll ever get one. Maybe once more styles of electric cars are available."

"Isn't Ramon the epitome of 'green'?" Joanelle laughed.

"It's admirable," Randall replied. "I'm project manager on the green energy plant near the airport."

"Cool," Ramon replied. "Isn't that coming online by year-end?

"My bonus rides on it," Randall laughed. "We are very close. I've worked killer hours the last four months."

"Yes, he has," remarked Sonya, putting her arm through her husband's. "I had to beg him to skip out to come here."

Ramon glanced at his watch. "Got to go. I got volunteered to help with face painting. The committee thought my minor in art history somehow qualifies me to paint kids' faces." He laughed. "Nice to meet you, Randall. I'd love to see that plant of yours once it's up and running."

"Sounds good. Good luck with the face painting."

Joanelle also glanced at her watch. At that moment, Herman Wilson and his spouse approached the group.

"Excuse me," Joanelle told the Marshalls. "Herman," she curtly said to her other co-worker, marching away.

"You'd think she'd let it go at Christmas," Herman said to Sonya.

"Don't worry about it, Herman. It's her problem. Everyone else has moved on."

Randall looked at his wife. She mouthed 'later' to him.

"I'm Herman, if you don't remember." He reached out his hand to Randall. "And this is my wife, Trudy. I think you and I met at this event a few years ago, before …" He paused, trying to find the words. "Before your son's illness."

"Yes, I remember now. Nice to see you again. But I'm sorry, I don't remember Trudy."

"We weren't together back then. My first wife had ... well, she was no longer in the picture. I hadn't been blessed yet to meet Trudy."

Randall looked over the couple. They looked like a perfect fit. Herman peaked at five foot four tall, he figured. Trudy was likely Joanelle's height. Herman wore jeans and a plaid shirt, untucked at the back as Lindsay had noted before. He could have just stepped off the tractor. The front of his shirt had food stains from tonight's hors d'oeuvres. A chunk of an appetizer had fallen into his breast pocket, partially still hanging out. Trudy's attire looked Mormon, circa 1850. She wore a conservative flower print dress, covered with an off-white smock or apron of sorts. The only thing missing was a bonnet.

"What do you do for a living, Trudy?"

"I work at a small rural bakery. All natural ingredients. Very healthy."

"Did you come straight here from work?" Randall asked.

"No, why do you ask?"

His wife kicked him subtly, hoping he wouldn't put his mouth further in his foot.

"I just thought you looked like you could have come from work."

"Oh, silly," she said, passing her hand in front of her face. "I get that all the time. It does look similar. My work smock is more colourful and has my name on it right here." She drew a line over her heart.

"I hate to run," Sonya said. "We need to find our kids. Enjoy the rest of your evening." She smiled, yanking her husband away.

Out of earshot, Randall asked. "What was that bit between Joanelle and Herman?"

Sonya looked around, pulling him aside. "Joanelle had a huge deal in the works. So big that Mr. Paul insisted that Herman help. He reviewed her financial details, finding some errors that he corrected. However, he made an error in his corrections in the final version that went to the client. He had increased the cost of the loan substantially. The client rejected it, taking their business elsewhere. Joanelle lost a customer, and a very fat bonus. He only gets small clients now. She's never forgiven him. Rumour is his tarnished reputation ruined his first marriage."

6 Visit with Santa

Sonya and Randall Marshall found their kids putting the finishing touches on their gingerbread house.

"I hope you managed to stay out of trouble over here," Mr. Marshall joked, popping in his mouth a black jujube from the decoration stash.

"We did, Dad," Benjay replied. "But some boy had the tube of icing explode all over his face."

"He squeezed it so hard near the tip that the back end burst open," Lindsay added.

"It was epic," Marcia added, laughing.

"Was the boy okay?" Mrs. Marshall asked.

"Yeah, he just laughed and ate the icing off his face," Benjay told her.

"His mother wasn't too happy though when she came to get him," Lindsay frowned. "It wasn't his fault and he still got in trouble. Said she was going to ground him. It wasn't fair."

Mrs. Marshall looked at her daughter wondering if she'd remember that moment the next time she was asked nicely, for the third time, to clean her room.

Mr. Marshall changed the topic. "Your gingerbread house looks awesome. Make sure you have them take your names, and we'll pick it up on the way out."

"No need, Dad." Lindsay grinned at her friend. "Marcia's taking it home. She promised Benjay and I can come over to eat it."

An announcement came over the microphone. "Will kids with tiles thirteen to twenty-four please come with their parents to line up for your visit with Santa."

"That's me, Mom." Benjay bounced up and down, with no need for a pogo stick. "We need to go! We need to go right now!" He started tugging on the sleeve of her blouse.

"Yes, dear," she smiled, gently removing his hand from her sleeve, and placing it in hers. She turned to her husband. "We'll find you. Wish me luck."

"I think the girls want to try their hand at some other games. Good luck." The three of them headed off.

Benjay yanked his mother's arm in the direction of Santa. "Why did you tell Dad to wish you luck? You're too big to sit on Santa's lap."

"That is true," she chuckled. "I meant to wish us luck that the line doesn't take too long."

The line to Santa only took about ten minutes, which made Benjay's mom happy. For him, the wait seemed forever. Some little kids cried once up close to the old, bearded man. Other kids seemed unprepared or nervous, not remembering what they wanted to tell Santa. Benjay felt nervous, yet confident. He'd recited his list in his head all day. He even said it out loud multiple times during his bath.

"Next," the cheery elf called. As Benjay approached, she talked to him. "My name is Snowflake, what's yours?"

"Benjay."

"Benjay," she smiled thoughtfully looking up for a second. "I don't think I've heard that name before. Just a few instructions. Please try to stay very still on Santa's lap. The other elf and your mother will be taking pictures. Limit your list to three ideas. Santa needs time to see all the kids tonight. Okay?"

"Yep, got it." Benjay smiled, moving toward Santa. The jolly man didn't seem as big this year, likely because Benjay had grown. He moved close and Santa spoke.

"Welcome, Benjay. Have you been a good boy this year?"

"Mostly," Benjay replied nervously, knowing he'd done a few things he shouldn't have.

"Mostly rates pretty good in my books, young man. Maybe you can do a little better next year, what do you think?"

"Absolutely," Benjay grinned.

"Let me help you onto my lap for the picture." With Benjay positioned and sitting still, the elf and his mom took pictures. The elf gave the thumbs up. "Okay," Santa said. "Let me hear your list."

"First, I want my dad's project at work to finish on time, so he can spend more time with us at home." He looked up at Santa, who nodded for him to continue. "Second, I want my mom to get her long-deserved promotion that she has worked ridiculously hard to get."

His mother blushed, recalling saying those words to her husband, thinking they were alone.

"Okay," said Santa, winking at Benjay's mom. "What else?"

"I hope Lindsay gets the new phone she talks about every second of every day. I don't want to hear about it anymore."

"I see," said Santa. "Nothing for you?"

"Snowflake told me I could only say three ideas, and those are the most important to me. They may be the hardest too."

Benjay's mother held back a tear.

"That's very generous of you, to think of others first," Santa replied. "And yes, some of those may prove hard for Santa to deliver. I'll see what the elves have up their sleeves."

Benjay leaned forward to Santa and whispered, though loud enough that others near the front could still hear. "I already mailed you my list. Your elves are probably already working on it."

"That's very good planning on your part," Santa grinned.

"Well, I better get going. You need to hear what these other kids want," Benjay said matter-of-factly, jumping off Santa's lap. "Merry Christmas!"

7 The Trip

Peepers bounced off the walls with the news that she'd see the machine-boy, Benjay. Fret had told her the news right after hearing it from his mother. She wanted to leave immediately. Fret said preparations had to be made first.

"It's winter outside," Fret told her. "We need to take precautions."

"Like what?" Peepers asked. "I've gone outside in winter before."

"Not for a few days, you haven't," he replied. "We have to get injections to prevent hypothermia."

"What's that? Is it a winter disease?"

"Sort of. You get so cold that you begin to get very sick. You can die if not treated."

"Don't want to freeze to death. We better get those. What else?"

"We need to get some instant food packets. Not much vegetation for us to snack on in winter."

"Don't want to starve to death. We better get those. What else?"

"We need to meet with Click and plan the trip. See when he can leave. I'm sure he's learning right now about the mission from an Elder, and that it's a priority."

"If we leave now ..." Peepers started to say, before cut off by her brother.

"It will be tomorrow at the earliest. We must wait a day for the injections to take effect."

"We better go get those right now, then!"

They headed to the doctor's office, getting right in. Fret got his shot first.

"Does it hurt?" Peepers asked.

"Not a bit," Fret replied.

The doctor poked Peepers with the shot. "Ow," she whimpered.

"Well, maybe a bit," Fret laughed.

"Okay, we're done. Let's go!" Peepers exclaimed.

"Not so fast, young lady," the doctor told her. "We need to keep you to ensure you don't have a reaction to the injection. It also says here that I need to do a full exam on both of you, and Click when he comes in."

Peepers groaned. "How long does that take?"

"Not long. You wait in the lobby while I examine your brother. He'll send you in when he's done."

Peepers frowned, moving to the lobby. Hovering back and forth around the room, she stopped to glance at pictures on the wall. She'd never noticed them before. They looked amazing. Staring at them made it feel like you were right there. One image showed Globe Celebration Day last year, another the flowery scenery by the old town bridge. A third one from the surface showed humans dancing in colourful costumes. She glanced at some small writing in the corner – "New Orleans, Mardi Gras,

Click." So, these were images that Click had taken. No wonder the Elders wanted him to get images of the human holiday. She'd never seen anything as vivid. It must feel amazing for him to recall things in such detail.

"I see you like my work," a Bubble asked from the far side of the room.

"Are you Click?"

"The one and only," he replied smiling. "I particularly like the Mardi Gras shot. It's good to think of the humans as passionate, happy people, rather than the images many of our history stories have portrayed of murderous barbarians."

"I agree, though I've met good and bad humans." Remembering her manners, she added, "It's nice to meet you. I'm Peepers." She looked oddly at him as his skin slowly changed colour. "Do you always do that?"

"You mean change colour?"

"Yes, that." He began to change again.

"Yes, unfortunately. It's a rare skin condition. The doctor says it's what makes me take such vivid images though. I guess it's a blessing."

"I've never seen that before. Then again, I'd never heard of you before this morning. Or noticed your work. I guess I never thought about somebody creating the images."

"That's okay. Most kids don't know my work, but the Elders love it."

"I do too. I wish they showed this stuff to us at school."

"That sounds like a great idea! Maybe when we return from this expedition, I can arrange a showing of the images at your school."

"That would be a great assembly!" She frowned, hearing the words come out of her mouth, thinking about Seer's words about Benjay at the assembly last night.

"Ah, yes," Click said, seeing her expression change. "The assembly. The primary reason for our trip. The machine-boy. You'll have to tell me all about him on the way there. It will help me with what to expect, and what pictures I can take."

"Fret says we're making a plan after the doctor finishes with us."

"Sounds good. I'm excited to see the boy."

"Not as excited as me... I just hope we have time to save him from the pending danger."

8   Behind the Tree

Benjay and his mother moved away from Santa and his elves, around to the side of the towering tree. A tall stack of gifts for the needy had accumulated on a couple of plastic folding tables.

"How did you enjoy your visit with Santa?" Mrs. Marshall asked her son.

"Cool. I was a bit nervous, but I didn't forget what I wanted to say," Benjay replied.

"You didn't look nervous. You were very generous with your requests, even if the one about me was a bit embarrassing."

"Don't you want a promotion?"

"Certainly. I've worked hard for it. I didn't want everyone to hear it though."

"Why not? How can you get a promotion if nobody knows you deserve one?"

"I'm sure Mr. Paul knows."

"Maybe he does." Benjay smiled up at his mother. "But have you told him yourself? Haven't you told us that 'you'll never know unless you ask'?"

Mrs. Marshall blushed. She didn't like to hear her own advice used against her by her children. "You know, Benjay? You are right. I will ask Mr. Paul on Monday. How's that?"

"Why not tonight? He's here."

"It's not the right place." She paused. "Well, it's the right place, just not the right time to discuss it at a company party. We shouldn't talk about work tonight. Understand?"

"I guess so."

"Good. Let's get back to your father and the girls."

"I have to use the bathroom first."

"That's a good idea." She put her arm around him, turning him to face behind the tree.

"Wow," he stated. "Is that the bank vault?"

"Yes, it is."

"Can you open the door? I want to go in and see all the money."

"Not tonight. It's locked down until Monday morning."

"Don't you have the combination? You're a big shot here, aren't you?"

She laughed. "I do, but the vault setup prevents it from opening at this time of night or weekends without an override from Mr. Paul."

"Oh," Benjay replied, glumly.

"Maybe another time, ok?"

Benjay perked back up. "That'd be great!"

"Alright. The men's room is to the right, the women's is to the left. I'm going to freshen up too."

"I'm not going to freshen up, I'm going to pee."

"It's an expression. It's more polite than saying 'I'm going to pee'. And women often touch up their makeup in the bathroom."

"That would explain why I've never heard Dad say that. He doesn't wear makeup. He just goes pee."

"Fine," she grimaced. "Let's meet exactly right here. Behind the tree. Make sure you wash your hands with soap and water for twenty seconds – count to twenty. Don't dawdle in there. And no wandering around afterward. Straight back here to this spot – wait here for me if I'm not here. Got it?"

"Got it," he nodded, though he wasn't sure he'd ever washed his hands for twenty seconds. He could count to twenty very fast. He ran through it in his head. 'Onetwothreefourfivesixseveneightnineteneleventwelvethirteenf ourteenfifteensixteenseventeeneighteennineteentwenty.' Five seconds by his best guess. Mom must count slow, he figured.

Coming out of the bathroom, hands washed and zipper checked, he hobbled a bit to the spot where his mother had told him. He knew when his leg ached that he'd been too active. It was Prosty's way of complaining. He looked in the direction of the women's washroom. No sign of his mother. He glanced around for a nearby place to rest. He didn't need a seat, just something to lean on. The gift tables – they stood the perfect height for him to lean on and were only a few feet away from 'x' marks the spot for waiting. At each end of the tables sat large Santa bags, stuffed with wrapped gifts. In line to see Santa, his mother told him those were fake presents that she'd helped to wrap a couple days earlier. He leaned back against the centre of the table. Feeling the table begin to buckle, he promptly stood up. He turned quickly to make sure the table wasn't going to collapse. Breathing a sigh of relief, he moved over to lean on the corner of the table, hoping it proved sturdier. It did, but he bumped up against the bag of fake presents, causing it to topple over. He jumped up, trying to grab the bag to prevent its contents spilling onto the floor. His hand caught the drawstring at the top, pulling it backward. His feet, however, tangled up in an extension cord on the floor, causing him to trip. Falling backward to the ground, he could see all the lights on the massive tree suddenly go dark as the cord went with him. He could hear the crowd in front of the tree let out a collective expression of disappointment. He looked up.

"Uh, hi, Mom," he forced a grin. "What's new?"

"Are you okay?" she asked.

"Yes, I think so." His mother was good at checking on his health before giving him a lecture about his latest behaviour.

"Good. Let me help untangle you and get the lights plugged back in."

By then, the elf Snowflake had circled to the back of the tree to see what caused the lights to go out. "Let me help you with that," she said to his mother.

"Thanks," his mother added.

"I'm just going to pull up your pant leg to help get this untangled," the elf said. Pushing up his pant leg, she paused, noticing his artificial leg. "Oh, I'm sorry." She looked at Benjay. "I didn't know."

"It's cool. Sorry to mess things up for you and Santa. Hopefully, he'll still get me what I asked for."

She laughed. "I'd say this still falls under the category of 'mostly good,' wouldn't you? I think you're covered." The cord removed from his around his limb, she plugged it back in. They could see the lights flash back on and the crowd cheer.

His mother helped him to his feet.

The elf picked up Santa's bag of fake gifts, repositioning it beside the table. "Right as rain," she smiled, patting Benjay on the head afterward.

"Why is rain right?"

"It's an old expression. Everything is normal since it's raining. Think it comes from England where it rains a lot."

"It's winter here and we expect snow. Should be 'right as snow'."

The elf grinned. "I like the way you think. Now excuse me, Santa needs me."

"Thank you for your help," Mrs. Marshall told her. "I'll pass a good word onto Mrs. Peters."

"Thanks!" She grinned at Mrs. Marshall. "Try to stay out of trouble, Benjay," Snowflake added, walking away waving.

9   Snacks

The Marshall clan gathered by the snack table, each holding a small Christmas paper plate with hors d'oeuvres. Mrs. Marshall's plate held veggies and dip. Everyone else's plates held an assortment of spring rolls, meatballs, pot stickers, and mozzarella sticks – except Benjay's only held meatballs. Marcia had left to hang out with her parents, happy with the prizes they'd won at the Snowball Bowling and Jingle Bell Pong. They'd chatted briefly with Mr. Paul and his granddaughter. Mr. Paul asked Sonya to see him while the kids decorated the tree. As Mr. Paul left, a young woman approached, accompanied by a young man in a wheelchair. They nodded at Mr. Paul as he passed by.

"Beatrice. Terrell. How nice to see you!" Sonya warmly greeted her co-workers. "Randall, this is Beatrice Hind. She joined us about, what was it, two months ago? Is it already two months?"

"Yes, hard to believe," she replied. "Is this your husband and brood?"

"Randall," he answered, "and Lindsay and Benjay." Randall shook her large hand. About the same height as him, she looked very young. He could tell she worked out by her muscular build. She wore her dark curly hair just below her ears, adding to her youthful look. "Nice to meet you, Bea."

"Oh, please don't call me Bea," she said, shaking her head, watching Lindsay snicker. "Your daughter, she gets it, don't you?"

"Yes," Lindsay chuckled. "Bea Hind."

"Bingo. I don't want to be the 'butt' of jokes if you know what I mean."

Lindsay laughed out loud.

"I'm so sorry, Beatrice," Mr. Marshall apologized, blushing.

Mrs. Marshall interjected. "And this is Terrell Bravo. I think you two started about a week apart, didn't you?"

"Yes, ma'am," Terrell responded.

"You're not in the army anymore, Terrell. Sonya is fine, remember?"

"Yes, m … Sonya."

"Terrell is an executive assistant to Mr. Paul. He's replacing Marjorie, who's retiring early next year."

Randall jumped in, looking at Terrell. "Marjorie – is she the one that's hard of hearing and, pardon me, kids, swears like a soldier?"

"That's the one. You know, they have placement training for vets. They teach us how to act in the workplace, that kind of thing. I'd worked hard to polish my speech to work as an executive assistant. The first time I met Marjorie, she let out a string of profanities that made me blush," he belly-laughed. "I'd repeat what I could remember, but maybe another time when your kids aren't here."

"Thank you for not repeating it," Sonya replied with a nervous smile, glancing at her children.

"What happened to your legs?" Benjay asked bluntly, without meaning to act rude.

"Land mine in Afghanistan, I'm afraid to say."

"Can't they give you new ones?" He rolled up his leg to show Prosty. "See mine?"

Terrell smiled, a slight tear creeping down his cheek. "I wish it were that easy. But yours is a beauty. Did you get yours in the war too?" he said, trying to be funny, hoping it would come off that way.

"No, I cut mine off shaving," Benjay replied. "Mom told me not to play with sharp objects."

The group burst out laughing.

"Cancer," Sonya stated. "He's finished therapy and went back to school late last spring."

"That's good to hear," Terrell said. "Say, you've given your leg a name. I haven't given my chair one yet. Do you think you could help me with that?"

"Maybe Wheeler. Let me think about it. I'll tell my mother any better ideas I get."

"Cool. Give me five, big guy." He held up his hand for a slap. "Enough about me, though. I think you need to give Beatrice the same third degree."

"Well," Beatrice started, "I'm the newest financial analyst. I took over for Ms. Doom, who suddenly quit. The first month was tough, I must admit. No transition plan, just 'here's your desk, get at it' from Joanelle."

"That's hard. Do you know why the other lady quit so suddenly?" Randall asked.

"She had some kind of accident. Told Mr. Paul she'd be safer in Florida with her parents. It seemed kind of odd, but whatever." Perkily, she added, "I got a job out of it, that's all that matters to me."

Randall looked at the two young employees. He wondered if they were in a relationship. They seemed to get along exceptionally well. He decided it best not to ask and face the wrath of his wife, or at least a kick in the shins if he was wrong. He shook both their hands again before they headed off to mingle elsewhere.

After they'd left, and the kids ran off to get another drink, Randall looked at his wife.

"No, they are not a couple. Thanks for having the sense not to ask. I didn't want to have to kick you with this plate of veggies in my hand."

"They look close. I guess it's their similar age and starting around the same time."

"They take lunch together sometimes, but Beatrice works long hours. She's pored over all kinds of old deals. Guess she's trying to learn how we structure them, and what kind of data she needs to prep."

"What about him? Is he a good worker?"

"Oh, my god – he's the best! I wish I had his energy and his organizational skills. He is so efficient that he gets Mr. Paul's work done and constantly comes around to ask the account managers if we need him to do anything. I'm glad to give him tasks." She paused to think. "Come to think of it, Herman does too, but Joanelle will never let him touch anything."

"Maybe she's afraid after the Herman snafu," he replied.

"Possibly, but it seems weird. There are a lot of little things like filing that he could do to save her time. But she gives him nothing."

"Her loss. I've met people like her before. They'd gladly work long hours simply to boast about how long they worked, like it's a badge of honour to be away from your family."

"What family?" she scoffed. "Sometimes I wonder if that Michael of hers even exists."

"You mean you've never met him either?"

"No, and Paul says he only met him once, when she first started. He insisted she bring him to his home for dinner."

"Oh, yes. I remember that 'meet the boss' dinner myself."

"It wasn't that bad. You know, if it wasn't for that mansion of hers, I'd think him a figment of her imagination. There's no way she could afford that without his inheritance and upper management salary."

The kids returned, more food on their plates.

"How much longer to the tree decorating?" Lindsay asked, looking at her watch.

"Should be any minute now. I'm sure they'll make an announcement soon."

Sonya caught Joanelle's eye, waving her over.

"So, these are your children." She forced a strained smile. "How delightful," she said as she noticed the sauce from Benjay's meatballs drip onto his shirt.

"Yes, Lindsay and Benjay," Sonya replied.

Lindsay did a mini curtsy, plate still in hand. Benjay mumbled a meatball 'hello.'

Sonya pulled Joanelle away for a private word. "I wanted to tell you what an amazing job you did with arranging Santa and the Elves. They are all excellent at their jobs. They really made the kids feel welcome and safe."

"Aw, thank you. That means so much to me. It really is hard to get good people these days." She cast a meaningful glance over to Herman Wilson. "They are a hand-picked crew. I'm sure they'll be amazing tomorrow too."

"Are they handing the gifts to the needy tomorrow?"

"Yes, the same crew. I've had them rehearsing for the past couple of weeks to be ready."

Sonya gave her a puzzled look. "I didn't think the job was that complicated."

"Oh, you'd be surprised. What to expect from the kids, from the parents, the timing of the activities, who's helping where and when. The event tomorrow became a show in itself."

"I had no idea. You make it sound like a theatrical production."

"A good play takes good timing. I learned that in my drama classes."

Sonya expressed surprise. "I never took you for the artistic type. Always thought of you as a numbers person."

"Even numbers require orchestration sometimes to ensure everything ties together."

"I suppose," Sonya replied, glancing at her watch. "The small-tree decorating starts in a few minutes. Paul wants to see me then."

"What for?" Joanelle barked, somewhat rudely.

Sonya took a half step back. "I have no idea. Likely wants to comment on the review of the Henderson deal that I handed in on Friday." She sighed. "He tells us no shop talk at the party. The rule doesn't apply to him, I guess."

"Ain't that the truth. Well, you better get going. I'm going to grab another coffee. I've got to stay afterward to supervise the cleanup and set up for tomorrow. Have a good night."

"You, too. Don't work too hard."

"I never work hard. I always work smart."

10 Tree Decorating

The announcement soon followed explaining the assignments for family tree decorating. The Marshalls got assigned the tree near the front, on the office side of the bank. It stood beside the stairs up to Mr. Paul's office. All the trees had lights and stringers, needing decorations and tinsel added. The trees were all to be lit simultaneously, upon completion of the decorating. Nearing their tree, the kids looked it up and down.

"What's wrong with this tree?" Lindsay asked. "It looks like it's dying."

Mr. Marshall looked around back. "It's right by the heating vent. Likely dried it out."

"It's fine to decorate. I'm sure the cleaning crew will water it tonight," Mrs. Marshall replied, then bid them goodbye to head up the stairs to her boss's office.

Mr. Paul sat in his high back leather chair, looking at a file in front of him.

"Come in, come in," he called, standing upon her arrival. "Would you like a glass of punch?"

"No, thank you. Just had some downstairs."

"Oh, this punch tastes much better. It's got some extra flavour if you know what I mean."

Sonya looked at him, a bit surprised.

"It's a benefit of being the boss. And major stakeholder. I always need a little something to get through these events."

"Okay, a small glass."

He poured her a couple ounces. "Good?"

"Perfect, thanks."

"I don't know if you heard, but that boy of yours drove me to extra pain reliever tonight," he laughed, holding up his glass."

"I didn't hear. I'm sure I'll ask."

"Don't make a big deal of it. Just the exuberance of youth, that's all."

"Is that what you wanted to see me about?"

"No, no. That's trivial. I have important items to discuss. Sorry to talk shop at a party."

She took a deep breath.

"Two things. One good, one bad. What do you want to start with? Your choice."

"You always tell us to look for the positives. Let's start with the good, then try to make the bad a good."

"Great answer," he laughed. "And the right one, too." He moved back to the punch bowl, topping up his drink. "Don't worry, my granddaughter is driving home."

Sonya laughed. "Will you both fit on her bicycle?"

"Good one,' he laughed. "Just kidding, her mother will drive us. First order of business. The good." He pulled a piece of paper from the file folder on his desk, reading it out loud. "For outstanding performance to Paul State bank, including loyalty, dedication, and hard work ..."

She felt her palms get sweaty. He continued.

"It is my pleasure to promote you to executive commercial account manager, level two, with a corresponding pay increase and granting of shares through the executive bonus program. Congratulations."

She held back tears as he handed her the paper, shaking her hand. The promotion put her at the same level as Joanelle, and above Herman, not that that mattered to her. "Thank you, sir. Thank you very much."

"Well deserved, Sonya. You hit it out of the park the past few years. This is, frankly, a little overdue. I'm sorry I didn't get to it early this fall, but that leads me to the other thing." He looked behind her. "Can you close the door and sit down, please?"

She did, and he sat in his chair, his expression now serious.

"We have a problem. We got an anonymous tip through a federal agency to review suspicious financial transactions. I need a detailed report for our board of governors meeting in late January."

"You don't suspect me, do you?"

"Do you think I would have promoted you if I did?" He laughed.

She shook her head. "Of course not. Silly of me."

"We don't know exactly what is happening. You've got the best mathematical mind on the team, and as I said, I trust you."

"Thank you, sir."

"Beatrice will assist you. She's already started poring through past deals, making great progress. She needs someone to help understand the details."

"I thought you'd show her," Sonya replied.

"I'm getting older, Sonya. I'm not as sharp as I used to be. This assignment will mean late nights. I can't work the extra hours at my age. You need to continue your day job to reduce suspicion. You also need to keep this confidential. The only three that know are me, you, and Beatrice."

"Got it. I'll talk to her on Monday."

"No, you won't. I don't want you to start on this until the new year. Beatrice will have everything compiled and questions for you by then. You have well deserved time off at Christmas. You need to spend it with your family, because come January, you may be here to all hours."

Slowly descending the stairs, Sonya folded her promotion notice, tucking it in her pocket. The tree decorations looked almost done.

"Mom!" I saved an ornament for you. "It's an angel. Like Daddy calls you, his angel."

She bent down, planting a gentle kiss on Benjay's cheek. "That's so sweet." She looked for an open spot and hung the glistening angel. She pulled out her phone to capture a photo of the ornament.

An announcement came over the microphone from one of the elves. "I think everyone has finished their trees. Let's light these babies up." Beside each tree stood an elf. They plugged the trees in one at a time, going clockwise around the large space of the bank. The attendees oohed and aahed, as they took videos and pictures. "That ends our celebration for tonight. If you made a gingerbread house, please pick them up before you leave. Safe travels tonight, and throughout the holidays. Happy Holidays!"

The crowd chanted back, "Happy Holidays!"

While other families lined up to get their coats, the Marshalls headed to their mother's office. She unlocked the door to let them in.

"Randall, can you and the kids wait here for a few minutes? There's something I need to ask Mr. Paul."

"Paul Paul," Benjay said.

"The fourth," Lindsay laughed.

Mr. Marshall chuckled with them. "Sure, hon. Hey kids, why don't you write out Christmas ideas on some paper."

Anticipating Benjay's response, he added, "I know you've sent yours to Santa. Mom and I would like to see your ideas too."

They nodded, sitting down.

Cutting through the lineup for coats, Sonya found her way to the stairs. Heading up, Joanelle passed her going the opposite way.

"He's all yours," she smiled.

Mr. Paul was putting on his coat, his granddaughter beside him already dressed for outside.

"Oh, I'm sorry to interrupt," Sonya said.

"I hope it's not about that new assignment. I told you, in the new year."

"No, it's not that. I forgot to say thank you for tonight. Such a wonderful event that felt even more special after having to miss the past few due to Benjay's illness."

"You are welcome, but you just missed the person who did most of the work."

"Joanelle. Yes, I thanked her earlier. Any problems? I just saw her leaving."

"No, she came by to remind me to be here first thing tomorrow to address the gathering for the underprivileged."

"Better you than me," she laughed. "I've got Christmas shopping with the kids on the agenda for tomorrow."

"Personally, I think better off here at the event than taking kids to the mall," he laughed back.

"Well," Sonya said, "I wanted to make sure to say thank you. Not all bosses would foot the bill for a night like tonight."

"It's my pleasure." He looked at his granddaughter. "Did you have fun tonight?"

"I had a ton of fun. Thank you, Grandpa."

"See," Mr. Paul said. "That's all that matters. Was there anything else? We have a car waiting."

"Nope, that's it. See you Monday. Good luck tomorrow, and good night."

11 The Ride Home

A light snow had continued through the evening, leaving a dusting of the white stuff on the car. Mr. Marshall brushed it off, his family sitting inside the heating and defrosting car. He stood by the car door, using the brush to remove snow from his shoes. Using his gloves, he swiped the minor accumulation off his head and body.

"Everybody buckled up?" he said once inside the car. After a round of yeses, he shifted to drive, pulling out of the parking lot. "Did you guys have a good time tonight?"

"It was awesome," Lindsay called out. "Marcia had a good time playing the games, and the prizes weren't 'el cheapo'."

Benjay didn't reply.

"You okay, Benjay? Didn't you have fun?" His father asked.

"Kinda. I didn't mean to hurt Mr. Paul," he spoke, looking down with a frown.

Mrs. Marshall reached back, patting him on the knee. "It's okay. He's okay. I saw him just before we left, remember. He was joking about it; not mad at all."

"Really?" Benjay asked.

"Yes, really. Exuberance, he said. That's all."

Mr. Marshall laughed.

Benjay twisted up his face, puzzled. "What does that mean to have extra uberance?"

"Exuberance," Mrs. Marshall grinned. "It means you have lots of energy."

"Not anymore. I'm tired now." He paused, grinning at his mother. "I did have lots of fun tonight."

"Did you thank your mother?" Mr. Marshall asked.

The kids looked at each other, smiling, then simultaneously belted out, "Thank you, Mom!"

She looked at her husband, silently thanking him for his appreciation. Then she remembered the folded piece of paper in her pocket. "Do you know what our son asked Santa for tonight?"

"Super Jet Flying Alien action figures?" Lindsay asked.

"No, but you would think so. He asked for three things." She glanced at her husband. "He asked for your project to finish on time, so you can spend more time with us."

His father grinned, fighting back a tear. "Thanks, son. We're getting very close."

She looked at Lindsay. "He asked that you get the phone you've been dying to have."

Lindsay patted Benjay on the head. "Thanks, little bro!"

"And last, he wished for me to get that promotion that I've waited ridiculously long for and deserve – his words, not mine. Well, they were mine, but not tonight."

Mr. Marshall snickered at Benjay repeating his mother, then added, "That was very thoughtful of you, Benjay."

"More than just thoughtful," his mother replied. "I got it tonight. I got the promotion! When Mr. Paul called me into the office, he gave me this letter. I moved up to level two executive account manager."

"I'm very proud of you," Mr. Marshall told her, reaching over to hold her hand. "You certainly did deserve it."

"That's great, Mom," Lindsay said.

Benjay repeated his sister. "Mom?" he asked, not waiting for a reply. "You said life wasn't like video games, but you just levelled up."

The rest of the family laughed.

"How about I put on the all-Christmas radio station, and we relax while your father drives us home?"

The kids nodded, knowing when to remain quiet. Five minutes later, both sat fast asleep.

"There's something else I need to tell you," Sonya semi-whispered to her husband, peeking backwards to see if her voice awakened the children. "It's about Mr. Paul calling me to the office. I didn't want to say it with Benjay awake, as he might get upset. Lindsay is older, she'll understand."

"What's wrong? Hard to imagine you'll be working more hours," he replied.

"Likely, that's why I didn't want Benjay to hear. He's asking for you to finish your project, so he has more time with you, and I'm going to be away at work longer."

"He just likes me more," he chuckled.

She gave him a light punch in the arm. "Seriously, though. I need to work on an investigation starting in January."

"Didn't you just have an audit in September?"

"We had a partial review, the bare minimum required by regulators. This is different. Mr. Paul will drive this investigation himself. They received an anonymous phone tip to look at the financials. He's very uneasy about it and must have it solved before the board meeting in late January. He's assigned Beatrice to work with me."

"Full time? I thought the financial analysts helped everyone."

"She's already working on it, under the guise of studying prior deals, how they are structured, and what data they need collected. I think she's giving Terrell some of her day-to-day work, to cover her true assignment. They both are very sharp."

"I thought so too," Mr. Marshall replied. "It's hard to tell from a five minute conversation that's not really work related." He looked briefly at his wife. "Something has bothered me though, from that conversation. What happened to the prior woman in the position? It sounded off to me."

"That's what I thought when I first heard. It was very weird how it all went down." She reflected for a moment. "You know, Lucy Doom started acting peculiar after her site visit to Tucker and Barnes Industrial Services with Joanelle. Lucy was never super perky, but when she returned, she seemed all ..."

"Doom and gloom?" he added, grinning.

"Yes, smart aleck. Definitely not herself. She didn't want to talk about anything. Like some big secret gnawed away at her, and if she spoke, it might burst from her lips."

"Something from the trip, you think?"

"Definitely, but I have no idea. I asked Joanelle. She said nothing happened out of the ordinary for a business trip. Oh, except Lucy had some issue with her suitcase on the way home."

"I could see losing a suitcase on the way there feeling super stressful, not having fresh work clothes, etc. But not on the way home."

"Agreed. Then, a week after they'd returned, a car hit her. Right out front of the bank."

"Ouch. I wondered what kind of accident would cause her to move home with her parents."

"That's the odd thing. Minor injuries only. The car glanced her and kept going. She got knocked down, but only had a bruised knee and slight ankle sprain."

"Doesn't seem like much."

"No," Sonya agreed. "The location of the accident bothers me most. It's a pedestrian crosswalk, with flashing stop signs and speed bumps on either side. Nobody goes more than twenty kilometres per hour on that road."

111

"They likely weren't going any faster than that," Randall countered. "If all she got was a few bruises, they couldn't be going too fast."

"Why did the driver take off?"

"Probably panicked. Maybe has a bad driving record."

"Maybe. I still feel like we're missing part of the story."

"Well, she's in Florida, isn't she? I guess you'll never know."

12 Full Moon Day

Peepers tried all night to sleep. Contrary to her thought the night before, last night was the full moon. Normally an afternoon sleeper, she was unaccustomed to the full moon glowing through her window when trying to sleep. Truthfully, she didn't think the moon kept her awake. With Fret the only one of her siblings not at school, and him sleeping in the other room, perhaps sleeping alone made her restless. More likely, nervousness or excitement about the trip kept her stirring endlessly.

"Rise and shine, little sister," Fret proclaimed, entering her room. He looked at her. Did he see bags under her eyes? "Didn't sleep well?"

"If not at all counts as not well, then yes."

"Since you're so tired, should I tell Mother that you're staying home?" He smirked, knowing full well that would never happen. He'd have to tie her down to keep her from going now, after she'd received permission.

"No. I'm ready." She grabbed a small bag with supplies. "Let's go."

They headed to the portal designated for their departure. Click waited, looking fully rested.

"Not sleep well?" he asked Peepers.

"Do I look that tired?" she asked.

"Sort of. Don't worry though, the cold air outside will perk you up instantly." He looked at Fret. "You've got the directions for our first stop?"

"I've got the general direction. Peepers will take us to the specific sites when we reach his town."

"Great! Let's go."

Hope met them nearing the portal opening.

"Mom!" Peepers called out. "Thanks for seeing us off."

"You look tired, dear."

"I'll survive."

"The Elders asked me to pass along their wishes for a safe trip. We'd prefer you come back tonight, but take up to forty-eight hours on the surface to make sure the boy is not in danger. Any longer and you'll need to come back for a booster shot before you can return, or we send another team if urgent. We certainly hope that the situation is not that grave, and perhaps Seer has misread the situation."

Fret and Peepers exchanged hugs with their mother.

"See you soon," Peepers told her.

Click was correct. The fresh air livened Peepers. Soon, she chatted Click's ear off about their adventure with the machine-boy. Click couldn't wait to see the boy, possibly even meet him. He'd never met or spoken to a human before. He'd taken lots of pictures of them, their activities and their lives, but Click had never been an active participant. At times it felt more like watching a movie about humans, rather than witnessing it.

115

His encounters lacked something – social exchange. He rarely got close enough to hear them talk, not wanting to risk exposure. He could get perfectly crisp images, zooming in from safe distances.

"That is an amazing story. No wonder you wanted to see him again," Click enthusiastically replied to her recounting. "Where to first, when we get to town?"

"The plant his father is building. That's where I first saw him. You said you wanted to communicate the positive side of humans. This plant is a step in humans reducing the pollution they put in the air. More of these plants would really help Bubbles."

13 *Sunday Morning*

The morning sun shone brightly through Benjay's bedroom
window, enhanced by last night's fresh coating of snow. Getting
home late last night, he forgot about closing his blinds. The
weather forecast had called for more snow today – possibly a lot
more snow – so sunshine surprised his sleepy eyes. Sitting up
slowly, he rubbed his eyes. He grabbed the pair of pants and
underwear he'd put on the nightstand before bed, as part of his
routine. On the edge of the bed, he slipped off his pajama
bottoms, sliding on the underwear. Grabbing Prosty, he slid his
pants over his artificial leg. Putting a shoe on Prosty, he slid one
pant leg over his good leg, attached Prosty to his stump, and
pulled up his pants. He'd tried different tricks, but this method
worked best for him. It rarely resulted in him falling. Buckling

his belt, he turned to make his bed, Benjay style. That meant the sheets and blanket were off the floor but not in a mound in the middle. He did a couple swipes to smooth the sheets, stopping at a lump. Pulling back his sheets, he discovered one of the prizes from last night's Christmas party. He smiled, remembering the fun he'd had. He chuckled to himself at the image in his mind of Mr. Paul doubled over from the bean bag toss. Since his mom said Mr. Paul was okay, he figured it was okay to laugh about it now. He reached for the bedroom doorknob, stopping to check his fly. Zipping it up, he opened the door and headed down to breakfast.

Sitting at the kitchen table, playing with his cereal as much as eating it, he heard his mother knock on Lindsay's door to get her up. Lindsay never had problems getting up on time, except on Saturdays. She enjoyed going to the early church service on Sundays, meeting her friends. While the Marshalls skipped church this week, something better lay in store for his sister today – shopping. She soon joined Benjay downstairs.

"You still eating? I heard you come down here ten minutes ago."

"Almost done. Besides, I can't fly down the stairs two at a time like you."

"That's true. But your cereal is a blob of mush that soaked up all the milk, meaning you're poking."

"Yeah, I guess you're right," he frowned.

"What's the matter this morning? I thought you had fun last night." She popped two slices of bread in the toaster. She looked at him, laughing. "When you nailed Mr. Paul, I could barely stop from laughing my head off. I mean the first time, with the bean bag. The second time in the chest with the hammer wasn't as funny, but that wasn't your fault. Not that you meant it with the bean bag," she stammered, trying not to make him feel bad.

"I had fun, but I'm not exactly crazy about shopping all day," he replied, just as his mother walked in the kitchen.

"You can't stay home playing video games all day," his mother told him.

119

"But Dad's home. And I'll play in the snow instead of video games."

"He's not home for long. He worked all night in his office while you guys slept. He's grabbing a few hours of shuteye now, then heading to the plant."

Benjay frowned, knowing he was too young to stay at home alone.

Their home phone rang. Mrs. Marshall grimaced whenever it rang, partly because it was usually somebody wanting to clean their duct work or scam them, but mostly because she kept forgetting to cancel the service. She looked at the caller ID. "Why would Marcia call you on our home phone?"

Lindsay shrugged. "Don't know." She grabbed the home phone. "Hello, Marcia. What's up? Oh, just a minute. Mom, it's Marcia's mother."

Mrs. Marshall took the phone. "Wendy, how are you? Good, me too. What's up? Oh, I see. Well, we can pick it up on our trip today. I need to pop in there anyway. Sure, no problem. See you later."

"What's up?" Lindsay asked.

"Marcia forgot her gingerbread house at the bank last night. Since her mom doesn't work at the main office, I said I'd pick it up."

She saw her daughter's look of displeasure.

"It's sort of on the way. Besides, I forgot my Christmas list at the office anyway."

"Yeah, we left our lists there too," Lindsay sighed.

"Can I bring the rolls of quarters that I've collected from doing chores?" Benjay asked.

"Afraid not, Benjay. The tellers aren't working today. It's only open to give out food and gifts to the needy." She glanced at her watch. "We better get skedaddling to make it before they close. I think the event ends at noon." She looked out the kitchen window, large flakes of snow beginning to fall. "Bring your warm gloves, scarves, and toques today. Just in case we don't get a close parking spot at the mall."

Within a few minutes, Lindsay had run upstairs, brushed her teeth, and come back down, hairbrush in hand. Benjay had brushed his teeth in the kitchen sink, a convenience his parents permitted to reduce the number of trips up and down the stairs with Prosty. He'd also used the main floor bathroom, washed his hands, and after almost forgetting, put the toilet seat back down.

"Ready?" Mrs. Marshall asked.

Lindsay looked at her phone. "Crap! My phone is almost dead. Let me grab my charging cord for the car ride."

Mrs. Marshall stood in the opening of the garage door, staring at the driveway. Some snow had accumulated but not enough to impair getting out of the driveway or around on the roads.

"It's coming down pretty heavy, Mom," Lindsay said.

"We'll be home by the time the worst of it hits. It looks bad, but there's not a lot of new accumulation this morning."

As they drove downtown to the bank, the roads slowly worsened for drivability. Not enough snow had fallen to warrant ploughs or salt trucks yet. They'd come out in the next few hours

122

for sure if this kept up. Another thought from yesterday came to mind.

"Kids?" she said, looking into the rear view mirror.

"Uh huh?"

"I forgot to show you something in the office yesterday."

"What?" Benjay asked.

"The secret passage in my office."

"No way!" Lindsay exclaimed.

"Yes, way. Way back when they rebuilt the bank, the owner's office sat where mine sits now, only bigger, using part of Joanelle's and Herman's offices. The bank used to get robbed a lot in those days. The owner put in a secret passage to hide or escape. If the robbers couldn't find the owner, they'd have to blow up the safe. Most weren't willing or able to do that."

"How do you open it?"

"There's a coat hanger attached to the wall behind my desk. You turn it clockwise until you hear a click, then push."

"Super cool," Benjay said. "Have you been in it?"

"Just once I peeked in, though a few times I thought of going in there to hide from Joanelle. She can get a little bossy sometimes."

The kids laughed.

"So, she doesn't know about your hideaway? Lindsay asked.

Her mother laughed. "I didn't tell anyone except Mr. Paul. He told me to keep it quiet."

"I bet it's all dirty and covered in spiderwebs, isn't it?" Lindsay asked, scrunching up her face.

"It was dark. If I remember correctly, it wasn't that bad."

"Where does it go?" Benjay inquired.

"I'm not sure. I didn't follow it. I don't know if it goes anywhere anymore. I remember standing on the outside of the bank, looking for a door that could lead from it. I couldn't find anything."

"Can we go in it today?" Benjay excitedly asked.

"Not today. We need to get to the mall and back before the storm." In the mirror she saw Benjay's shoulders droop. "Maybe next Saturday we can come back to check it out. Deal?"

"Absolutely, one hundred and ten percent deal!" he proclaimed.

14 Back to the Bank

Mrs. Marshall pulled into the side parking lot reserved for employees. It had closed the night before to those that didn't get their name pulled in a special draw. The lot wasn't big enough when all employees showed up at once, which only happened at the Christmas event and other fundraisers. "Darn," she said. "That truck is where I usually park. Must be from the helpers that Mrs. Peters hired for the event." She looked around, finding an open spot slightly further from the door.

Getting through the revolving door without incident, or the need for the security guard, they entered the massive bank. The setup from last night mostly remained, with tables for food, the beverage stand, and most of the games. The gingerbread and cookie decorating stations had been removed.

"Can we play the games, Mom?"

"We don't have time, son."

Benjay frowned, until he looked around seeing all the kids sporting smiling faces, holding their new toys on the teller side of the bank. Their parents stood with them, the elves serving sandwiches and hot chocolate. About five kids were still waiting in line to get their gifts.

"I think they put any forgotten gingerbread houses in the employee lounge. It's the room between the safe and the women's washroom. Can you guys run and get Marcia's house? I'll open my office to get the lists."

"Sure," Lindsay replied, grabbing Benjay's hand to pull him along. He yanked his hand away.

"I'm not a little kid."

"Sorry," she laughed. "Old habits."

Heading to the back of the bank, they saw Santa giving out gifts. Circling the large Christmas tree, they spotted the employee lounge. Benjay stopped for a second. The vault was open. He wondered why it was open. The bank was closed for the party. He'd have to ask his mother, he thought. In the lounge, Lindsay lifted the gingerbread house before Benjay could put a hand on it.

"I'll carry it," Benjay volunteered.

"Oh, no you don't. You are a little prone to accidents."

"I don't mean to be."

"That's why they are called accidents. I'm not going to have an accident wreck Marcia's gingerbread house. Follow me."

They filed out of the lounge, Lindsay a couple steps ahead of Benjay. Beginning to circle the tree to head to their mother's office, she heard a crash behind her, followed by a groan from everyone up front. She turned to see Benjay tangled up in the lights again. This time, he quickly untangled himself and plugged the lights back in. The elf that approached stopped short with the return of the lights, heading back to her duties. She didn't notice the large Santa bag that Benjay had knocked over.

"Linds! Get over here, quick!" he called to his sister.

"You'll have to pick it up yourself, Mr. Accident. I have my hands full."

"I know," he said, straightening out the bag. "Look what's inside."

"I know what's in the bag. Fake presents that Mom helped to wrap."

"That's what supposed to be in there. But it's not!"

She nudged closer, not wanting to get too close with the gingerbread house in her arms. Her eyes popped open. Inside she could see jewels along with many bundles of money. "What?" she exclaimed, before quickly clamping her mouth shut, worried she had blurted it out too loud. "Put it back. Quick. Let's get away from here and talk to Mom."

Benjay straightened up the red bag. He put the single remaining fake present back on top, pulling the draw-string tight. He nodded at Lindsay, and the two of them quickly walked to see their mom. Just before entering their mother's office, they could see Santa had finished handing out gifts. Along with the elves, he now talked to the remaining guests at the food tables near the front door.

Then it happened.

Beside the rotating door stood a large swinging door that security had unlocked to allow the kids to get out easier with their gifts. Through the door came three people in long trench coats, wearing masks, and with guns above their heads.

"Everybody put your hands up where I can see them!" the tallest one yelled to everyone in the bank, pointing his weapon at the security guard. He disarmed the guard, ripping his radio from the holster. He also took the man's cellphone.

The second robber, slightly shorter with broad shoulders, simultaneously yelled at the others in the bank while approaching the group near the food tables. "Keep those hands up. I'm not afraid to use this thing," he continued to yell, waving his rifle around. He spotted an elderly lady without her hands in the air. "Get them up!" he yelled at her, before raising his rifle and shooting three bullets into the ceiling. The woman slowly, and painfully, raised her hands as best she could. "Good. Now throw your phones and purses this way." He moved his weapon back and forth, watching the group closely. "Don't try anything stupid."

The third robber, the shortest and slimmest of the three, moved away to look for other people in the bank.

Lindsay stepped into her mom's office, put down the gingerbread house and reached for her phone in her back pocket. It wasn't there. She'd left it charging in the car. She grabbed her mother's phone off the large desk and quickly began texting.

"What are you doing?"

"The bank is being robbed. I'm sending Dad a message. Sent." She handed it back.

"Quick," their mother told them. "Get in the secret passage. Now."

"Cool," Benjay said.

"It's not a game, Benjay," his mother told him, opening the door to the hiding spot. "You two stay as quiet as you can, understand. I'll let you know when all is clear."

"Be careful, Mom," Lindsay whispered as the opening in the door disappeared. The new room swallowed them in near darkness. A small ray of light shone just above her eye level. She balanced on her tiptoes to peek into an eye hole. She could see most of her mother's office! She watched her mother quickly sit down, flipping open a file on her desk, pretending to work. Lindsay could hear the slightly muffled conversation.

"You," one of the robbers said from the doorway. "Throw me that phone and get out here."

She complied. Her purse remained on the floor out of his sight. He shoved her phone into a bag with others he'd collected.

He motioned to the group near the teller stations. "Go sit over there with the others!"

15 The Search for Benjay

Descending to the surface, the Bubbles emerged from the cloud

cover to a world of falling snow. Peepers had only gone to the

surface in the winter a few times. The falling snow still

marvelled her, looking like magic, and tickling as it bounced off

her skin. The tickling sensation wore off as the intensity of snow

increased. She'd seen and felt snow before, but she'd not seen

flakes this big.

"The plant where Mr. Marshall works is this way, just

ahead."

The Bubbles flew in close formation to avoid losing

sight of each other in the gusting snow.

Floating near the roof of the plant, they slowly

penetrated the building's ceiling in transparent mode. Performing a slow pass of the different areas of the facility, they saw no sign of Benjay or his father. Fret signalled to the others to leave the way they came.

"Let's try the school," Peepers told them. "It's about time for his lunch break."

Approaching the school, they saw no signs of life. No kids, not even any cars or buses.

Fret shook his head. "Today is Sunday for them. I forgot that they don't go to school on Sundays. Shall we try his house?"

"Can we wait?" said Click. "I want to go into the school. The kids would enjoy some images of holiday decorations at a human school. Won't take long, promise."

Fret nodded, remembering the two parts to their mission.

Peepers wasn't too happy but didn't object.

In a few minutes, Click reappeared, smiling. "Got some great images from different classrooms. We're good to go. Lead the way, Peepers."

They quickly arrived above the Marshalls' house.

"Benjay's room is on this side," Peepers pointed. "I think we start there."

"Okay. Let's go invisible so we don't startle them," Fret added.

Peepers led the way, followed by Fret, then Click.

"Oh, wow," said Click, entering the empty room. "This is amazing."

Peepers watched him. Click stared at something, blinked his eyes, then moved onto the next thing. He repeated this process five or six times, then announced he'd finished.

Next, they checked the bathroom. Fret kept Click from playing with the water devices. They didn't want to alert anybody to their presence. From there, they went to Lindsay's room. Also empty. They floated downstairs, searching the kitchen, den, bathroom, and living room with no luck.

"I don't think anyone is home," Click said.

"We're not done yet. Two more rooms on this floor, then downstairs," Peepers informed him.

"They live below ground too?" Click asked, surprised.

"Sometimes," Peepers replied. "You two look in the last room up here. I'll check for Benjay playing below the surface."

The two male Bubbles entered the room to a sleeping Mr. Marshall.

"At last," Click replied. "But this doesn't look like the machine-boy that she described."

"It's not," said Fret. "It's his father. I didn't think the adults slept during the day, though."

Peepers returned, shaking her head 'no' to finding Benjay. "What now?" she whispered, looking at the sleeping man. As she asked, something vibrated, lighting up on a table next to the bed.

"Ugh," Mr. Marshall grunted, reaching behind him for the device. Patting the table a few times, he located his phone. Pulling it close to his face, he rolled over, then sat up. "Rubbery?" he said, scratching his head.

The Bubbles hovered above, moving closer to read the phone. Peepers wasn't paying attention and knocked over a lamp from the table at the other side of the bed.

Mr. Marshall jumped up, looking around. "Crap," he said, looking at the dishevelled sheets on the bed, assuming he'd somehow tangled them up in the light cord and pulled the lamp over. He moved around the bed, picking up the lamp to return it to the table. He sensed something and slowly looked up.

Fret slowly turned visible.

Mr. Marshall stepped back. "Fret?"

"How did you know I was here?"

"I don't know. I seemed to sense something. It felt odd."

"Interesting," said Click, making himself visible, followed by Peepers.

"Peepers! Good to see you." Mr. Marshall looked at Click. "I don't think I know you, do I?"

"Click. And no, we haven't met. You're my first human. I mean first human to talk to."

"I see," said Mr. Marshall. "Nice to meet you. What are you three doing here?"

"We're looking for Benjay."

"He's gone to the mall with his mother and sister." He looked at his watch. "It's probably been an hour or two by now. What do you want him for?"

Fret cleared his throat. "I'm not sure how to say this…"

"We think he may be in danger," Peepers blurted out.

"What? Why?" Mr. Marshall asked.

"It's hard to explain," replied Fret.

"The Seer told us," Peepers bluntly said. "She had a vision."

"What are you saying? That a fortune teller said my son is in danger?"

"She's more than what you call a fortune teller," Fret replied. "She's definitely different from what you have down here."

"Well, it's still hard to swallow." Mr. Marshall glanced at his phone again.

"What's bothering you?" Click asked.

"This message from my wife." He held up his phone. "Bank rubbery."

"Do you have banks made of rubber?" asked Peepers.

"No," Mr. Marshall laughed. "You sound like Benjay sometimes." He paused, and suddenly his face went ghostly pale. He picked up the phone, pressing his wife's number.

"What's wrong?" Fret asked.

"I think she meant bank *robbery*," I'm calling to check on her."

The phone rang through to voice mail. He hung up, texting a reply: 'Everything okay?' He waited. A couple of minutes later he placed his phone on the bed. "I'm going to jump in the shower to think this over."

Fret looked at him. "People need to have water run over their heads to think clearly?"

Mr. Marshall laughed. "Not all the time, but sometimes it helps after sleeping. I'll see you in five minutes." He grabbed some clothes and left for the adjoining bathroom.

"I've never seen a shower before," said Peepers.

"No, you are not going to watch," Fret ordered her. He looked at Click. "And no images by you, either. Humans like their privacy in the bathroom, for some reason."

Emerging from the bathroom half clothed, Mr. Marshall rubbed his hair with a towel. He ran his fingers through it to tidy it a bit, then grabbed a shirt from the closet. He picked up his phone. No response to his text. "They were supposed to go to the mall. I can't see them texting me about the bank in the mall. She must be talking about her bank. I got it. I'll call her office phone." He dialled. "No answer there either. The bank is normally closed on Sundays. Maybe she got called in to help with the charity event." He rubbed his chin. "I'm going to have to go downtown to her work, in case she's in danger like you suspect."

"Lead the way," said Fret. "We'll be right behind you."

"I can't ask you to get involved. It might be dangerous."

"That's exactly why we must help. It's our orders."

"Your orders?"

"Yes, the Elders said we must protect Benjay Marshall," Fret said gravely.

16   The Bank Robbers

Sonya Marshall sat on the floor of the bank near the front doors, legs crossed. She thought back to her training about bank robberies. Stay calm. Cooperate. Observe. Avoid eye contact with robbers. Don't be a hero. She repeated the steps several times in her head. She had cooperated. She'd stayed calm, so far anyways. Her kids were safe, making it easier to remain calm. Next step was to observe. She remembered not to make eye contact – something about it making the robbers nervous, like you were trying to identify them behind the mask.

Looking around, she wondered where everyone had gone. In the group with her sat the kids and parents remaining from the gift giving. None of the elves or Santa were with them. Where were they held? And why keep them separated? The lone robber watching them stood at the other end of the group of hostages – she thought about that – she was a hostage! The stocky robber flirted with an attractive mom at the opposite end of the group, where they'd also placed the security guard. The other robbers mostly remained out of sight. Every two minutes, the tallest robber would come from behind the large Christmas tree, do a loop in front, then return from where he came. She assumed he was perimeter control while the third robber worked on opening the safe. She guessed the third robber to be the brains of the trio, as he obviously wasn't the brawn, being much smaller in stature than the others. The safe was an older model, its outdated security features one reason Mr. Paul had confidentially discussed relocation. If the second robber stopped his rounds, it likely meant they'd gotten into the safe and the two of them had begun loading up loot for escape.

A thought came to her mind. It seemed like an odd robbery from what her course had taught. Most robbers simply held up tellers for cash, often with a note and no visible weapons. The tellers weren't even open today, being a Sunday. Plus, they usually wanted to get in and out as quickly as possible. That meant they targeted the vault. When it came to safecracking-type burglaries, she'd always thought they occurred in empty banks at night. The robberies had bigger crews to disable alarms, monitor police activity, get the loot out quickly, etc. Likely a movie stereotype, but why rob it on a Sunday, with people in the bank, knowing the safe had to be cracked? And only three people? Were they greedy, wanting bigger cuts of the take?

Observing the robbers, she noted they all had the same black trench coats, masks, boots, gloves, and guns. She could make out part of a tattoo on the neck of the broad shouldered one watching the hostages. A bird of some sort, she thought. Yes, an

147

eagle, as he shifted his weight. Definitely an eagle. She tried to nonchalantly look at the other robber during his next loop. He had his collar rolled up. Maybe he did it to cover the same tattoo? It might help the detectives track the robbers down after they left. Nothing else distinctive could, but again, they were mostly covered head to toe.

A jumble of thoughts ran through Sonya's head. Getting worried about the kids holed up so long, she just hoped the robbers would get it over with and leave. She thought about asking to use the women's room, to get a better idea of what was going on. Her thoughts got interrupted.

"Hey, look at the little peashooter they gave this guard." The robber near her called out to the one making a loop. He waved the gun around. "It probably doesn't even shoot straight." He pointed the gun toward the decoration at the top of the tree and shot at it, missing. "See, told you!"

"Put it back in the bag, you moron!" the other robber yelled at him. "Before you hurt yourself. You're supposed keep

these nice people calm and quiet, not scare the crap out of them."
He shook his head. "You better hope the boss doesn't reduce
your share for acting stupid."

Sonya put the idea of snooping out of her head. She
reminded herself again of one of the rules: don't be a hero. At
least she knew the one working on the safe was the boss. She
continued to wonder about the elves and Santa, then she asked
herself a question. If they'd been moved to another room, like
the employee lounge, was robber number two, who circled the
tree, watching them? And if so, who was watching them during
his loop? Surely, the safe-cracker, the boss, wouldn't interrupt
his work to watch them every two minutes. She wondered.
Maybe they were barricaded in the lounge. But how? The door
pushed in with no lock that she remembered; it would be hard to
barricade from the outside. If the others were not barricaded in,
what did that mean?

Her train of thought got interrupted by the clicking of
high heels on the marble floor, coming from the other side of the

149

tree. She looked over to see Joanelle walking toward her office. Sonya had forgotten all about Joanelle being here to oversee the event. It was good to see her safe and unharmed. The second robber walked behind her, holding his gun at his side. Joanelle paused briefly in front of Sonya's office, then glanced over, seeming surprised to see Sonya, but acting like she hadn't seen her. She continued toward her own office. The robber stood outside her open door while Joanelle disappeared from Sonya's view inside the office. Less than a minute later, Joanelle returned with her purse in her hand. She'd likely convinced him that she needed a bathroom break, and knowing her, she made a stink about not going to the bathroom without her purse to freshen up. Hopefully, the bathroom break was a ruse to survey the situation. Joanelle and the robber disappeared behind the large tree, heading to the back. Joanelle was likely held with the elves and Santa. Sonya felt encouraged that somebody who knew how to remain calm in this situation was with them. She just had to keep her own calm, watching the time tick by on her watch.

17 Hiding Out

Standing in the hidden corridor behind the offices, Benjay's hands started to feel cold. Minimal heat from the offices seeped through the old walls.

"You doing okay, little bro?"

"Hands are a little cold. I'll tough it out. Glad we kept our coats on. Wish I didn't leave my hat and gloves in the car. How 'bout you?"

"Okay, all things considered," she replied, stepping away from the peephole. For the first time, she looked around the space they occupied. She could see similar pinpricks of light on each side of her, one for each of the offices. Five in total. If she remembered from the 'Bring Your Kids to Work Day,' on the left from here was Mrs. Peters's office, then one for all the financial analysts. To her right stood Mr. Wilson's office, followed by a smaller one for Mr. Paul's assistants, with a workstation for consultants or head office staff to use when they visited (or her on 'Bring Your Kids to Work Day'). The men's bathroom lay beyond that at the right – she felt happy to see no peephole light coming from down there!

"Looks like you can peep into each office from back here." Lindsay moved to the side with Joanelle's office. "Nobody home. They must have put her with Mom." She moved to her right. "I don't think Herman had to come in today. I'll take a quick look. Nope, nobody."

"Can you give me a boost? I want to see, too."

She complied, though she hadn't realized how much her brother had grown. She couldn't lift him easily like last year. She dropped him after a few seconds.

"What you do that for?" he objected.

"I'm obviously not as strong as I was last year," she grinned slyly at him.

"Oh, so you're calling me fat. I saw you lifting those big snowballs yesterday."

"You are heavier than a big snowball, but you are definitely not fat, Benjay Marshall. Not that it would matter. You're just growing."

"What's our plan?" Benjay asked, satisfied with her answer.

"Our plan for what?"

"To rescue Mom and stop the bank robbers."

She laughed, cupping over her mouth. If she could hear people on the other side of the wall, they could likely hear her. "We wait it out. That's the plan. Nobody usually gets hurt in bank robberies if everybody lets them go about their business. That's what Mom told me."

"It sucks that the bank robbers get away with it."

"They often get caught, just afterwards, not during."

As she finished her thought, they heard a gunshot.

"OMG!" Lindsay exclaimed. "Did you hear that? Sounded like a gunshot, at least what they sound like in movies."

Benjay nodded, scared.

153

"I think we need a plan after all." She paced back and forth down the dark hallway.

"What about we go running out into the bank, yelling and screaming. You know, create a division."

"You mean diversion? And no, that's an awful idea. They'll just shoot us to get us to shut up and keep the others in line."

"Oh." Benjay frowned. "I don't like any plan where we get shot." He started to pace behind Lindsay. She quickly turned around, bumping into him. "Any ideas yet?" he asked, seeing her unhappiness at the collision.

"A couple, let me think some more." She began to pace; he continued to follow.

"We could go all 'Home Alone' on them," Benjay offered.

"I'm not sure that's a great idea. You can think about what we could do in case we get desperate."

Encouraged by his sister's response, Benjay stopped and closed his eyes, thinking about everything at their disposal in the bank.

A few minutes later Lindsay stopped pacing. She moved in front of the peephole for their mother's office. "I've got a start," she told her brother as she looked around her mother's office through the eyeball-sized window. "Do you think you can push this door closed, if I go out and come back in?"

"Sure. It doesn't look heavy like the revolving door. What are you planning?" He rubbed his hands to warm them.

"First thing is to get Mom's purse from behind her desk. While it doesn't have her phone, she always has that pen flashlight, plus paper and other stuff we may find useful. Maybe we can find another way out of here that we can't see right now in the dark. I also noticed she's got a one-step stool for reaching books at the top of her bookshelf. You can use that to peep through these holes."

Benjay beamed at the thought of his sister thinking of him.

"Okay," she said, peeping through the hole. "I'm going to open the door then hide behind her desk. You close the door behind me. I'll get the purse and stool, then open the door when I think the coast is clear. Ready?"

155

"Yup."

"Here goes. Remember, close the door right behind me." She pulled open the door just wide enough to squeeze through, then bent over and raced to hide behind the desk. Turning back, she saw the door close promptly. She took a deep breath. She pulled the purse close, turning her attention to the stool. Just around the chair and back. She didn't think she could be seen by anyone in the hallway by staying low. She crawled to the stool, grabbed it then paused, thinking she heard a noise in the doorway. She lowered her head to peep under the desk. A pair of women's shoes paused briefly in the doorway before moving away. She exhaled. Positioned behind the desk again, she braced herself to bolt for the secret door. She closed her eyes to remember how her mother opened it. Turn the coat hook and push at the same time. Got it. She peeked around the desk. The doorway and into the bank looked clear. She pushed the stool and purse close to the secret door and opened it, scampering through. Benjay had apparently listened intently by the door; he tumbled backward at her quickly opening it. She tossed the purse and stool through, grimacing as she heard the stool clank loudly on the floor. She

pushed the door shut, not waiting for her brother to get back up.

She quickly peeked out of the hole. She gasped at what she saw.

Mrs. Peters stood in the doorway, looking into their mother's

office. She wasn't held hostage with their mom. Why? Was she

one of them?

18 The Corridor

Lindsay sat on the stool in the hidden corridor, catching her breath. Her mind raced, wondering what was going on in the bank.

"Maybe somebody had a gun to her back, and you couldn't see them?" Benjay offered an explanation.

"Maybe," she said, still thinking. "You said you saw the safe open earlier, right? Before the bank robbers came in."

"Yep. Mom says they don't open it on weekends. Only Mr. Paul can override it. I didn't see him here, did you?"

"No." Then she chuckled. "But I didn't even notice the safe open when we walked right by it."

"Mom says you don't pay attention too well."

"I just find my phone more interesting than you guys, sometimes. Too bad I didn't have my phone this morning to blame for not seeing the vault open."

"What about the Santa bag with the loot in it? We saw that too before the robbers showed up."

"Maybe somebody prepared the loot ahead of time for the robbers to take, so they wouldn't take as long. Like an inside job," Lindsay pondered.

"Then how come they aren't gone yet? Wouldn't they just grab the bags and run?"

"Maybe they need to take time to make it look like they are stealing the stuff themselves, and that there is no inside man. Or it could be they have more stuff to get out of the safe still. What we need is to get a look at what's going on."

"I think it's too risky for you to go into Mom's office again," Benjay said, concerned.

"Likely." She pulled the pen flashlight from her mother's purse. She shone it down the corridor, first toward the front of the bank, then the back. "Let's look around here. I think there must be another exit."

"Yeah, let's look. I think the bank manager in the old days likely wanted to escape, not just hide."

Lindsay nodded agreement, pointing the light toward the back. "Let's go slow to look for hidden doorways."

Scanning the inside and outside walls, they easily saw the doors to the other two offices at this end. Nothing they could see on the outside walls. They continued. No sign of a hidden door to the men's bathroom. They kept looking along the outside wall until they hit the end.

"Dead end," Benjay moaned.

Lindsay shone her light around. "Maybe …" she shone the light on the interior wall. "This kind of looks like a door here."

"There's no light. No peephole," Benjay said.

"Maybe there is." She shone her light about her eye height, seeing an opening, but no light. "It must be covered on the inside. You can see the outline of a door here." She shone the light up and down. "Look, here's a handle."

161

"They likely coved it because it's a bathroom."

"The robbers aren't likely to be in the bathroom. I say we open it and look around."

"Okay. You open it. I'll go in. If someone looks in, they'll just think I'm one of the kids here for the event."

Reluctantly, she agreed. "I'm going to leave it partly ajar. There may not be a handle on the other side." She pulled the door open and Benjay stepped around it.

"Linds, come look."

Confused, she pulled the door open wider. The doorway had been blocked by a shelving unit loaded with packages of toilet paper and other cleaning supplies.

"If we move a couple of things, I think I can squeeze through," Benjay told her, taking off his coat. He began pulling supplies into the corridor. With a fair-size gap created, she shone the light through, but couldn't see much. He began to wiggle through, then fell with a slight thud on the floor. "I'm in."

"Duh," she replied. "What do you see?"

It wasn't the bathroom. Benjay flicked on the light to look around.

"Turn it off!" Lindsay loudly whispered. "Somebody might see the light from the bottom of the door."

He turned it off. "Janitor's room, by the looks of it."

She leaned into the hole, shining the penlight around. "Yeah," she agreed. "Supplies too." The light hit the back wall. "Another door! Looks like it goes outside. They likely use it to load supplies. This room must sit beside the vault."

"Do you want me to peek outside?"

"No!" she cried out. "See the sign above the door? It has an alarm. We might get out okay, but Mom would be stuck, likely with angry bank robbers, knowing someone got away to warn the police." She looked around a bit more. "In fact, you should get back in here. We don't want you to get caught." At that moment she shushed him. "Did you hear that?" she excitedly whispered. "Footsteps!"

Benjay paused long enough to hear them, before scampering through the shelves blocking the opening in the wall.

163

Lindsay haphazardly shuffled supplies on the shelf, then quickly closed the door. Peering through the peephole, she realized her line of sight remained blocked. She quickly reopened the door, shifted some items to allow them to see through the peephole, then pushed it shut quickly but quietly. Though it was dark inside, they could at least peer in.

The tall robber opened the storage room door and flipped on the light switch with his gun, which he quickly returned to shooting position.

"Someone in here?" he shouted. "Come out now, with your hands raised," he barked.

Lindsay covered Benjay's mouth in the secret hallway, muffling his heaving breathing caused by crawling through the shelves. She slowly moved her head to glance through the peephole.

The robber pushed a few supplies around different parts of the room, looking for any place somebody could hide. Comfortable that nobody could possibly be hiding in the room, he turned toward the door. He suddenly stopped, staring directly at the peephole.

Lindsay rapidly ducked her head, moving slightly away from the hole in the wall. She firmly placed a hand on Benjay's shoulder, informing him not to move.

The robber leaned forward as he approached the wall, squinting as he drew nearer. He slowly pushed his finger toward the hole and through it.

Lindsay sat up straight holding her breath as the finger poked through only inches from her head. She would have loved to lunge and bite the wagging digit but thought better of it.

The man yelped as he pulled his finger back.

Lindsay quietly wondered if she hadn't just thought it, but had actually bit it.

"Ouch!" the robber exclaimed. "Great! A stupid sliver." He sucked on his finger momentarily before muttering under his breath, "I'll never get that sucker out of there." He punched the wall. "Stupid mouse holes." Leaving the room, he shut off the light and closed the door behind him.

Lindsay could hear the man wiggle the doorknob, ensuring it was locked from the outside. With the storage room deserted, she let out a huge breath and heavy sigh. Benjay did the same. "That was way too close, Benjay. My heart was racing up a storm."

"Mine, too," her brother replied, "like a gazillion beats a second."

Flicking on her penlight, she looked at Benjay and laughed. He had dust streaking from his feet to his head, with a dab even on his nose. "You look like you cleaned under your bed with your body." She dusted him down from his Zamboni slide through the shelves. "Let's go see what mysteries lay at the other end of the corridor."

They hustled down the hall, quickly coming to the other end.

"Look, another door!" Benjay called out, spotting it at the end. "I don't remember another room at the end, just the stairs."

Lindsay grabbed the handle, pulling. It didn't budge. She put her muscles into it, feeling slight movement. Another hard pull resulted in a crack emerging by the handle. "Come here, Benjay. Put your hands on the edge of the door and pull when I do." She moved to let him duck under her arms. They pulled together a couple of times, gaining an inch or two each time. Eventually, the door opened wide enough to see in.

"I don't think this has been opened in forever," Lindsay said, pulling the light from her back pocket. She shone it inside. She looked around for a few seconds then pulled her head back out. "It looks like a small room under the stairs. I don't see any other doors or way out, only a few very old looking wooden boxes. And spiders. Lots of spiders." She shivered her shoulders in disgust.

"Spiders aren't that bad," Benjay replied. "Let me look." He took the light, peeking in. He pulled his head back out. "That is a lot of spiders! Big spiders, too." He reached to hand her back the light. It flickered weakly. "Looks like our light is dying out, sis."

She grabbed it. "Close your eyes."

"Why? You're not going to put one of those spiders on me, are you?"

"Ugh, no. I'd have to pick one up to do that. Just close them."

He did so.

"Okay open them," she said after ten seconds.

"It's dark. You turned the light out."

"Yes, while your eyes were closed so you could adjust easier."

"Oh yeah! Cool, I can see pretty good already. I'll have to remember that trick when Mom turns my bedroom light off at night."

"Let's go back to behind Mom's office to come up with a plan now that we know the layout. We better act quickly."

19 The Ride Downtown

Mr. Marshall notified work that he had a family emergency, without getting into details. He opened the garage door, groaning at the sight. The snow had begun to accumulate on the driveway. He didn't like backing out on fresh snow. It left tread marks that proved much more difficult to shovel later.

"It's going to take me a few minutes to clear the drive," he told the Bubbles.

"Let me help," volunteered Click. "You want a path from here to the road?"

Mr. Marshall nodded.

"Ok."

Fret looked at Peepers, not sure what their travel partner had in mind. Transparent to view, Click flew the length of the driveway. He looked for observers, while measuring the length. Back at the garage, he lay on the threshold, spreading himself thin across most of the door opening.

"You should cover your eyes. Or look the other way."

They shielded their eyes, then heard a 'click.' A bright light emitted from Click's body, rolling down the driveway like a wave. The snow melted, then disappeared completely. At least for the moment; new snow continued to fall.

"Wow," Peepers cried out afterward. "I've never seen anything like that!"

"That was amazing," Mr. Marshall added. "I could use you around here all winter," he laughed.

"Just some light generated with heat. The hard part was controlling it. Burned down a lot of my parents' shrubs practising that trick."

They laughed getting in the car.

"It may take some practice getting used to travelling in one of these cars. It can be easier to just follow it on the outside, if you prefer," Fret warned Click.

"It's up to you. Once we get going, the car will be nice and warm," Mr. Marshall said, trying to entice them inside.

"I'm riding inside, so I don't have snow blasting in my face as I fly," smiled Peepers.

"I'll try riding inside," replied Click.

They all flew into the car, and Benjay's father began to back out. It took Click a few minutes and a few partial exits from the vehicle to get the hang of it. He was happy once he did.

"Mr. Marshall," Fret asked, "What exactly is a bank robbery, and what do we need to do to ensure Benjay's safety?"

"Good question. A bank robbery is usually where bad people try to take money that isn't theirs from a bank. People put their money, jewels, and other valuables in a bank to pay bills, save money, and for safe-keeping. Amongst a whole bunch of other reasons."

"It sounds like it's a crime to rob a bank," Peepers said. "We don't have much crime."

"You are lucky. Some of these robbers can get violent. If there is a bank robbery, they'd be going after the safe. Which

171

means they will have guns and may have explosives to open the vault."

"That does sound dangerous," Fret said. "How do we keep Benjay safe?"

"I have a plan, or at least the start of a plan," Mr. Marshall said. "When we get to the bank, can one or more of you go invisibly into the bank to make sure there is a robbery going on? I don't want to file a false report with the police. You'll need to do some reconnaissance, like how many robbers are in there, how many hostages, do the robbers have guns? That kind of thing."

"Yes, we can do that," replied Fret.

"I don't want you interfering in any way. Just go in and report back. Got it?"

"Yes."

"Good. Once you confirm it is a robbery, I can call the police and give them the information. They can decide how to proceed."

"How do we help after checking things out?" asked Peepers. "We want to help out."

"You can probably go back in to keep an eye on Benjay, Lindsay, and my wife."

"Do you want us to fly them to safety?" Click asked.

"No, but thank you. They could get hurt if you try it. You could put the lives of the other hostages at risk, whether you are successful or not."

"We will try," Fret replied. "But if we feel Benjay is in imminent danger of harm, we will act."

"And I am glad that you are here, just in case," Mr. Marshall responded, somberly. "Let's hope that isn't necessary. For everyone inside."

20   The Plan

The plan was simple, and the first part went off without a hitch.

Using the small note pad from her mother's purse, Lindsay wrote

a brief message. Something her mother could read quickly

without getting noticed. She found a hair tie in the inside pocket

of the purse, handing it to Benjay to hold. They headed to the

secret door to the financial analyst's office. She headed in,

checking that this door had the same opening mechanism as her

mother's door. She nodded to Benjay. He closed the door behind

her. She knew that just outside this office sat a Christmas tree

and the stairs on her left. The Santa Bag Toss lay on the floor to

her right. She edged up to the doorway to see if the coast was

clear. One bank robber stood with their back to her, to the far

right of the hostages. Her mother sat close to the front doors at the opposite end of the group. Lindsay crawled into the doorway, reaching around on the right until she grasped three of the Santa bean bags. Extras, in case she missed. She pulled them back into the office, sitting up, her back to the wall. She strapped the note to a bean bag with the hair tie, tugging it to make sure it stayed snug. She glanced around the corner to see the robber still facing the same direction. She quickly pulled her head back as a second robber emerged from the far side of the tree. She could hear him loop around in front of the office she hid in. She tried to stay as quiet as possible, holding her breath. Hearing the footsteps move away, Lindsay knelt in the doorway, bowling the bean bag with all her might in her mother's direction. With the bag on its way, she stepped back into the office, near her escape route. The bag bounced up against her mother, who snatched it, tucking it under her sweater. Her mother looked in her daughter's direction. Lindsay was unsure if she'd been seen prior to slipping back through the door. Her mother would know who it came from without reading it.

"Thanks!" Lindsay said to her brother once the door closed behind her. She looked through the spyhole. The angle wasn't right to see her mother. "Now, let's collect the stuff we need from the supply room."

They made their way to the other end of the hallway. Checking the coast was clear, Benjay squeezed through the shelving into the dark supply room.

"It's really hard to see in here," Benjay complained to his sister. "You sure I can't use the light?"

"Okay," she relented. "But keep the light away from the door – and be quick!"

"Thanks," he said, flicking on the light. He plucked a few items off the shelves, passing them through to Lindsay, who stacked them in the corridor. She turned back, blinded by light.

"I told you not to turn on the light!" she whispered as angrily as she could.

"It's not," Benjay replied, the light going out. "I found flashlights. They must have them in here for emergencies."

"Good eye, bro. Grab extras. Did you find anything with the flammable sign on it?"

"How's paint thinner?"

"Perfect. Get that and get out of there. That flashlight shines bright enough, they might see the light under the door."

21 The Santa Bean Bag

Mrs. Marshall quickly seized the miniature Santa bag. Spotting a note attached, she grasped the note, stuffing it in the front of her pants. She recognized what held the note in place – one of her hair ties. She shoved the tie into her pocket, waiting to read the note. Too much movement at once would possibly draw the eye of the robber on guard. The gun happy one. Waiting a few minutes, she slipped the note out, spreading it on the ground between her legs, obscured from anyone else's view. She waited for what felt an eternity before glancing down to read the first part.

'Safe. Benjay saw safe open before robbery.'

She looked up toward the robber again, covering the note with her foot. She absorbed that sentence before reading the remainder. Why would the safe be open today, she wondered. Why would Mr. Paul override the weekend lockdown? What could he possibly need out of the safe on a Sunday? Bank agreements and pending deals weren't kept in there. Everything was online. She took a deep breath, then read the rest.

'Saw loot in Santa bag also before robbery.'

That just sounded too wild. Benjay must be making stuff up again. That boy had a wilder imagination than his grandfather, and that was saying something. Did he make up the part about the safe being open? Why would he do that? Surely, Lindsay would have told him the seriousness of the situation and that now was not the time for a fairy tale. She glanced at the note. It was Lindsay's printing, such as it was. Seems they didn't teach kids in school how to print or write anymore, she sighed. Lindsay wouldn't write it down if she didn't believe it. Plus, Lindsay had to have thrown it. Benjay would have either come up short with his toss or thrown it twenty feet wide – he struggled with certain tasks with Prosty, throwing being one of them. She heard he fell last night trying to throw too hard. He

180

likely would have fallen right in the middle of the bank today. She laughed to herself, then wiped away a tear.

She continued to think things through. Assuming she believed Benjay, because Lindsay believed him, what did that mean? The loot he referred to had to come from the safe or safety deposit boxes. If it was there before the robbery … was someone robbing the safe before the actual robbers showed up? An inside man? Were they preparing the goods for a speedy getaway? No, that couldn't be it. The robbers would have finished by now. Unless they were completely clearing out the safe. That would take some time. Either way, Mr. Paul had to open the safe. He was supposed to get here first thing in the morning for the ceremony. She hadn't see his car in the lot, but she'd been distracted by Santa's truck. Maybe that truck was the getaway vehicle. No, that couldn't be right either. It was here before the robbers, too. They must have their own getaway van. A horrible feeling swirled in her gut.

Mr. Paul was the inside man.

22 Reconnaissance

Mr. Marshall pulled the car into the same lot as the night before.
It lay deserted, except for his car. Parking was free on Sunday –
a bonus, he thought. He reviewed the instructions with the
Bubbles. They flew off to investigate.

Exiting the car, Fret reminded his young sister Peepers
of the rules. She had a habit of conveniently forgetting, or
stretching, the rules from time to time to her benefit. He told her
it was no time to do her own thing. Lives were at risk.
Surveillance only.

The three Bubbles entered the bank from the front near
the ceiling. They travelled together to compare notes upon return
to the car. Fret led the way clockwise around the building. He
made note of Mrs. Marshall sitting with the hostages up front,

guarded by a robber with a rifle. Nobody behind the counters on that side. He marvelled at the large, decorated tree, hoping Peepers wasn't only staring at that. They dropped down to examine a few rooms near the back on that side, a washroom, and an empty room with tables. The next room had a very thick steel wall. Going through that depth of wall would take a lot of energy. It also meant making that last push to get through would probably result in them popping into the room. Hard to remain invisible and avoid detection when that happened. They took the easier route around the front, between the large tree and the steel-walled room. As they did, a second human with a rifle walked right under them – a narrow miss. In front of the thick steel door to the room stood a third human with a rifle. Inside, a flurry of activity occurred. The room had a couple of walls covered with little metal doors. One human broke the doors open while others emptied the contents into bags. A woman stood in the corner, and a man sat in the corner on the floor, possibly asleep. They didn't stay to look any closer. Flying at human height to see into the room put them in danger of detection. They

184

moved onto the rooms on the other side of the building. They quickly went through those empty rooms, making their way out the front to report to Mr. Marshall.

At the car, they went through the details.

"Your wife is safe, at the front, but under guard," Fret reported. "We didn't see the kids. Are you sure they are with her?"

"Absolutely." He scratched his chin. "Go on, while I think."

"Are you going to need another shower, so you can think?" Peepers asked.

Mr. Marshall grinned, but shook his head 'no'.

"Three robbers with guns," Fret continued. "A whole bunch of people emptying the little boxes in the steel wall room at the back."

"That's the safe."

"It doesn't seem very safe," Peepers frowned. "There is a robber with a rifle standing by the door."

"Are they making hostages empty the boxes?"

"I don't know. They all had unusual uniforms on. Green and yellow, with pointy hats," Fret replied.

"And cute little shoes that curled up," Peepers smiled.

"One male hammered open the little boxes. He must be the boss because he had on a beautiful red suit."

"That's a Santa suit," Mr. Marshall snickered. "Doesn't mean he's the boss, though he could be. I better call the police. I need you to go back in to find my children. Perhaps they are hiding."

"We can do that," Fret replied. "I'd like to find Benjay and get him to safety away from the guns."

"Before you go, and I call the police, do you remember anything else?"

"Yes," Click answered. "There were two other humans in the safe not wearing outfits like that. A woman stood in the corner, standing beside a man that sat in the corner."

"Mrs. Peters and Mr. Paul!" exclaimed Benjay's father. "She organized the event. He must have come to give a speech or something. Did they look okay?"

186

"They did," replied Click. "Do you want to see an image?"

"Do you Bubbles have cameras?"

"Click is a flying camera," Fret grinned.

Click brought up a small image of Mr. Paul.

"He looks like he's been knocked out," Randall Marshall stated. "Can I see the other one?"

Mrs. Peters appeared on the dashboard.

"That's her alright." Mr. Marshall squinted, moving closer to examine the picture. He pulled back. "Any chance you can make it bigger or zoom in on her hands?"

Click enlarged the picture, then zoomed in.

"What do you see?" Peepers asked.

"A gun. Mrs. Peters is holding a gun."

23 Options

Mrs. Marshall tried to remain calm. If she had a pen or pencil, she'd write a note back to Lindsay. Just as well, she thought. The robbers would either catch her throwing the bean bag back or catch Lindsay trying to retrieve it. The kids were better off hiding. They'd remain safe so long as the robbers didn't know they were in the building. She'd just have to stay patient. Surely, the robbers must be getting ready to leave soon. She forgot to check the time of her capture. Thirty minutes had to have passed by now. Were the robbers trying to get in the Guinness Book of Records for the world's slowest bank robbery? She chuckled to herself – she'd have to remember to tell the kids that.

Lindsay looked through the peephole into her mother's office.

"Did you feel that?" Benjay asked her.

"Feel what?"

"A chill. I just felt a chill. I felt it a few minutes ago, too."

"It's just from hiding in the cold corridor for so long."

"I guess. My hands are pretty cold." He rubbed them together, wishing he'd looked for gloves in the supply room. "How are we going to help Mom?"

"I've got a few ideas, but they are dangerous. I'm not sure Mom would be happy with us getting involved."

"Can we go through the ideas we came up with? I only remember the toilet paper one."

"Of course, you remember that one," she laughed. "Ok, in no order. We'll figure that out. Burning tree – we set the dry tree near the front on fire as a distraction, and hopefully set off the fire alarms."

"That's a good one. What else?"

"Toilet paper – starting rolls, then launching them from the balcony to the floor below. Just a distraction." She looked at her brother. No response. She continued. "Heist – we steal one or more of their large Santa bags of loot. Confuse them and maybe turn them against each other."

"I think we'll get caught on that one. Those bags are too close to the safe."

"You're likely right. The bags are likely heavy too. The distractions could help though."

"I thought we had another one," Benjay inquired.

"Drone. From Mr. Wilson's peephole I could see a toy drone still under the tree. Mom said there may be extra presents that would go to a shelter tomorrow. Distract them with a drone flying around."

"Trying to get it from under the tree would prove hard. Too bad we didn't have a drone already that we could fly out there to snatch up the other drone."

Lindsay laughed. "Genius. But why would we need to do that if we already had another drone?"

Benjay frowned. "Oh yeah." He perked up. "If we had two drones, they might be strong enough to bring the Santa bag to us."

Lindsay shook her head, rolling her eyes. "Let's review again. Fire, toilet paper, bag heist, single drone. What do you think?"

"I think fire," Benjay replied. "They may just think the bulbs caught the tree on fire."

"They might. That tree is almost completely brown. Do we agree that the heist is too dangerous? The fire isn't a distraction to rescue Mom, it's just to hope the fire alarm goes off."

"Yep. How are we going to light it?"

"Mom's got a lighter on her desk."

"Why? She doesn't smoke."

"Some client gave it to her. It's a fancy crystal looking thing. Mom said it made a pretty paper weight. I'll sneak in, grab it, and bring it in here. We'll use the paint thinner to light a bean bag on fire, then toss it at the tree from the end office."

192

"Won't you catch your hands on fire?"

"Good point. We'll have to come up with some other way to handle the bean bag."

"I'm glad it's you doing it. Mom would ground me until I'm ten for playing with fire."

"Don't you know it! Let's go, before I chicken out. Or come to my senses."

24   Outside the Bank

Outside the bank, an unmarked police car and a cube van pulled into the parking lot near the Marshall family vehicle. An officer escorted Mr. Marshall to the rear of the oversized van with the doors open, exposing high-tech gear around its walls. Stepping up into the van, he stopped suddenly. Terrell Bravo, Mr. Paul's executive assistant, occupied a station on the side. Beatrice Hind sat near the front inside wall. She removed one side of her headset to talk.

"I'll explain." She motioned for him to sit. "We're working undercover for the FBI Financial Crimes unit, investigating a tip we received indicating financial irregularities with Paul State Bank."

"You mean someone has been stealing money."

"In simplistic terms, yes."

"You don't think it's my wife, do you? Is that why you got assigned to work with her? To shadow her?"

"Not at all. We know she's not involved. She is very good at her job. She'd help me dot the I's and cross the T's on my investigation. Close all the loops to ensure a conviction."

"That's a relief. Who do you suspect?"

"I think you know that, from the information that you shared with the officers."

"Joanelle Peters!"

She nodded. "Her lifestyle is too extravagant for her income."

"Her husband ..."

"Does not exist. No travelling the globe for work. No inheritance from his mother. He's a cover story, that's all."

"Wow." He paused. "I thought he went to dinner at the Pauls' when she first hired on, like his initiation to the bank?"

"She brought somebody, but it wasn't a husband. Likely an actor she knows. She's an ardent supporter of the local theatre."

"What are your next steps here? My family has been in there a long time."

"We know, Randall. Any chance you are willing now to explain how you got your intel on the activities inside?"

He crossed his arms. "I'm sorry, but I can't explain. I'm sure your team has seen," – he looked at the equipment actively monitored around him – "or at least heard what's going on in there."

"We tried linking into the bank's cameras. Unfortunately, their security system is outdated." She paused. "We'd feel better if we knew about your children. We're writing that off as incomplete or incorrect intel," – she looked him in the eye – "from whomever your source is."

Mr. Marshall grimaced, knowing she would withdraw immediately and treat it as a hoax if he divulged Bubbles as his source.

"I'm sorry," she continued after no revelation of his source, "but we can't treat this as a robbery and call for re-enforcements until we are able to confirm the situation for ourselves. I'm sure you understand."

Mr. Marshall nodded.

Beatrice looked at the agents with headphones on. "For now, we listen to the chatter. We're hoping to confirm the situation is as described. We'll listen to confirm the number of perps involved, where they are located within the building and, if we are lucky, hear their next move. Once we have some of that data, we'll summon SWAT or local enforcement, or whatever is needed."

Mr. Marshall sighed.

"It won't take as long as it sounds," Beatrice replied to his angst. "If anything goes south inside, we won't hesitate to act. Ideally, we'll be able to set up and catch them coming out, rather than us having to go in. Less confrontational, and safer for all involved."

"Okay." He leaned back. I guess we wait here and see."

"*We* wait here, not you," she said looking at Terrell and her other technician. "Randall, please go back to your car – and stay put. Got it? Any attempts at bravery may jeopardize the entire operation." She stared him down. "And your family's wellbeing."

"Understood." He left the van to sit in his car.

25 Mayhem

Hidden from view in the corridor, Lindsay grabbed one of the spare bean bags from her earlier trip, securing it to a broom handle with hair elastic ties. She opened the paint thinner. Benjay gagged at the smell with her as she poured the liquid, saturating the bean bag.

"It's making my eyes water," cried Benjay.

"I better get going before the smell makes us sick," his sister said, coughing as she resealed the paint thinner. Armed with her mother's decorative lighter and the stinky bean bag on a stick, she entered the office closest to the front of the bank. She hoped the hair ties held, now wondering if she should have used cleaning rags to hold the bean bag in place. Confirming the coast clear, she lit the bean bag, reached around the outside corner of the office, and tossed the bean bag, broom handle and all, at the dry Christmas tree. She didn't stay to see the result. She heard a powerful whoosh, followed by screaming from the hostages. She slithered on the floor back toward safety in the hidden corridor.

The broad shouldered robber at the front of the bank performed a cursory glance at his hostages. Starting with those closest to the back of the bank, he looked them up and down as he strolled by. He tried to establish eye contact with each hostage to ensure they knew he watched their movements. He held his rifle near his shoulder to show he controlled the situation and to remind them not to make a break for the door. He really didn't want to have to shoot a hostage, though it would be an effective deterrent to the others. Nearing the front of the bank, a flash over his shoulder caught the corner of his eye. He quickly turned to see one of the Christmas trees burst into flames. On the ground near the door to one of the offices, he spotted something moving. He pivoted, lowered his rifle, and let loose a barrage of gunfire in that direction, splintering the wooden door frame and riddling the wall with holes.

"Just this last row of safety deposit boxes and we're done, ma'am," the man in the Santa suit reported. He readied to break a lock on another box.

"About time!" She looked at her watch. "That took much longer than planned." She turned to the third robber, who'd been standing guard at the vault door. "Tell the other two up front that you leave in five."

Turning after the robber left, she started to bark at Santa, "Hurry up with that last …". Before she could finish, a loud noise erupted from the front of the bank, followed by a burst of gunfire. "What the heck was that?" she exclaimed, her face turning red with rage. "Go check that out!" she screamed at one of the elves, seconds before the fire alarm blared. "Oh crap!" she murmured to herself. She raised her voice above the alarm. "Get those three clowns up front out of here – NOW!" she belted out as loud as she could. "Everybody else, stop what you're doing

and pack up."

26 Injured

The Bubbles had hovered out of view examining every square metre of the bank. Still no sign of Benjay and Lindsay.

Until the tree caught fire.

"There," Peepers whispered to her companions, her exceptional eyesight in action. "I just saw Lindsay at the door of that office."

"Let's follow her," Fret replied. "Benjay must be with her."

They headed to the office, pausing as a human fired a weapon repeatedly into the opening Lindsay had just crawled through.

When the gunfire stopped, they quickly flew to the office. Empty. "I'm sure it was this one," Peepers said, confused as she frantically looked around.

"Me too," said Click. "I saw somebody go in here, and this is the one the human shot bullets at."

"Look for hiding spots," Fret replied. "And quickly, the humans will likely come after her."

Click slowly scanned the room. "There!" He pointed at the back wall. "There is a trail of liquid leading to the rear of the office. I think there may be a hidden door in the wall."

Not waiting to be told, Peepers flew into the wall, emerging on the other side in front of a shocked Lindsay. Fret and Click joined immediately.

"Peepers?" Lindsay said, drawing the attention of Benjay, who lay on the ground, breathing heavily.

"Peepers!" he exclaimed. "What are you doing here?"

"We are here to rescue you," Fret answered. "Good distraction, with the fire. We need to get you out of here."

"Take Benjay," Lindsay replied, crying. "One of the bullets came through the hidden door and struck him." Blood soaked the sleeve where material frayed, a result of a bullet ripping through his coat. "Does it hurt, bro?"

"A little," Benjay weakly smiled.

She pulled off his coat. "It doesn't look bad," she said, not really knowing what a bad bullet wound looked like but figuring there would be arm guts showing or something. "There's not a hole in your arm or anything. I guess that's a good sign. Just glanced your arm, I guess."

"That's goob," Benjay whispered, the trauma affecting his speech.

She tightly wrapped a cleaning rag from the supply room around his arm.

"Owww!" Benjay cried out loudly, before his sister tried to muffle the sound. The last thing they needed was to be overheard by one of the robbers outside the corridor.

"Sorry, the cloth needs to be tight to prevent bleeding."
She looked up at the watching Bubbles. "I need one of you to
help me with something before you leave."

"We can't get your mother out, I'm afraid," replied
Peepers. "Too many witnesses."

"It's not that. It's to foil the bank robbers."

"Okay, I'll stay," volunteered Click. "I'm Click, by the
way."

Fret nodded. "We'll come back once Benjay is safe with
his father, in case you need help." He and Peepers surrounded
Benjay, carefully transporting the wounded boy through the
outside wall to safety.

27 Police!

"There's a fire inside!" agent Hind cried out. "And gunfire. How far out is the SWAT team?"

"Less than two minutes away, ma'am," Terrell responded.

"What about local police?"

"First two cars just pulled up. Two more en route." He looked at his screen. "And fire rescue should be here about the same time as SWAT."

"Not ideal, but we'll make it work." She hopped on her radio to the local police, suggesting they encircle the front door as best they could with the limited resources currently on site. "If some suspects exit the bank before SWAT arrives, you may need to apprehend and clear the area. SWAT will need to further assess the situation before fire rescue can enter the building."

The two police cruisers and the unmarked vehicle moved into place and the officers took cover behind their cars. Moments later, three robbers came through the large door, each with a large Santa bag draped over their shoulders and their rifles hanging by their sides. They obviously hadn't expected the police to be there.

"Police!" boomed a microphone from behind one of the cruisers. "Drop your weapons and get on your knees!"

Two of the three robbers dropped their bags and their weapons and fell to the ground, putting their hands behind their heads. The third, stockier robber, lifted his rifle to shoot, but quickly fell to the ground screaming as a bullet struck his shoulder.

Click got his instructions from Lindsay. They moved down the corridor, toward the end with the safe. They stopped behind Mr. Wilson's office. Click zipped through the wall, not waiting for Lindsay to finish opening the passage door. Spotting his targets, he grabbed one. Lifting it, he switched from invisible mode to flashing like a multicolour strobe light. He rushed the bag to Mr. Wilson's office, then headed back for another. Then another. Lindsay pulled the heavy bags through the secret door into the hidden corridor. After three bags, she told him to stop. It was enough – besides, she didn't want Click to get caught.

"What on earth happened out there?" the boss asked the elf as she returned.

"One of the trees caught fire."

"The brown one near the door?"

She nodded.

"I wanted to torch that pathetic thing myself. Lights probably saved me the effort. What about the gunfire?"

"That trigger-happy lunatic thought he saw something near the tree."

"Likely a mouse," the boss replied. "We've got a few of them around this old place."

"Did the three of them get away okay?"

"They were heading out the door last I saw."

"That's not what I asked," she glared at the elf. "Never mind, I'll check myself." She huffed before leaving the safe, walking around the large tree to look out front. "Crap!" she yelled, running back to the vault. "The cops nailed the three of them out front," she told Santa and the elves. "Change of plan," she cursed. "Make sure the crew and all the loot are here in the vault. We need to close the door." She looked over at Mr. Paul. "And chloroform the old guy in the corner again for me. I want to make sure he's unconscious until tomorrow afternoon."

Santa took a couple elves to retrieve loot bags from behind the tree. He didn't know how many red bags the elves had stuffed, but it seemed less than he thought as he watched the elves run back and forth. He started to return to the vault before stopping in his tracks. He thought he saw one of their loot bags moving across the floor by itself before flashing lights blinded him. Maybe he shouldn't have carried around that chloroform in his pocket all day – he'd started to hallucinate.

28 The Escape

Outside the bank, the police handcuffed the three robbers. The burly one cried police brutality over being handcuffed after he'd been shot. He didn't get any sympathy. The robbers' bags of loot were confiscated and taken to the cube van. Fire trucks, sirens screaming, pulled up out front and their crews disembarked, ready for action.

"You better come here, ma'am," one of the SWAT team called to Ms. Hind.

"What have you got?"

"It's not what we have. It's what we haven't got." He pointed at the bags. "They are empty. Well, not empty. They have fake presents in them. No money. No gold. Nothing of value."

"What?" she said, staring at the bags, temporarily puzzled. "Good to know. Good work," she thanked the officer.

She looked at the front of the bank, relieved to see the hostages pouring out unharmed as the SWAT team aided their exit. Smoke accompanied them out the door into the cold, snowy air. No flames remained visible behind them. She turned, hearing a boy holler "Dad!" as he came around the corner of the building.

"Benjay!" Mr. Marshall called out, running from his car. "You're hurt!"

"Lindsay says it's only a flush wound."

Mr. Marshall chuckled as he examined his son's arm. "Flesh wound, big guy."

Ms. Hind rushed to join. "Where is your sister?" she called out to Benjay.

"She's still inside."

"Where did you come from?" she asked. "And don't say you were with your mom. I saw you come from the side of the building."

"That's where I came from."

"How did you get out?"

"A friend helped me out?"

"Who might that be?"

"I can't say."

Ms. Hind looked at Mr. Marshall. "Did your informant have something to do with this?"

"Maybe," he said.

She grunted. "I'll deal with you two later. Take your son to the paramedics. We've got to finish this rescue, and hopefully recover your daughter. Unless, of course, your informant takes care of that too," she said sarcastically, storming off.

Beatrice Hind entered the bank to talk to the lead of the SWAT team.

"The robbers locked some hostages in the vault. We don't know how many, but the other hostages said it must be all the elves and Santa."

"The elves and Santa, eh?" She sighed deeply. "Can't wait to write this one up. Mystery informants, kids appearing out of thin air, elves, and Santa."

"How do we get them out of there, ma'am?"

"Go find Mrs. Marshall, one of the hostages. She works here. She'll know. I'm hoping this isn't locked down until tomorrow morning."

"Yes, ma'am."

"Wait!" she called him back. "You're sure there is no way out of the safe, except this door?"

"Yes, ma'am. We've done ultrasound on the walls, floor, and ceiling in this area. They didn't blast or tunnel their way in, so no way out either."

"Excellent," she replied. "And Joe?"

"Yes, ma'am?"

"Take your time. I want the occupants to sweat it out a bit in there."

29 The End

Beatrice poked her head in the door.

"Sonya, we need you now."

Mrs. Marshall called the security company to get the emergency vault code. Mr. Paul remained knocked out inside the vault, per Mr. Marshall's mystery informant. While they waited for people with the required security clearance to get on the line, Sonya caught up on events.

"So, you are a federal agent? Wow. I suppose your real name isn't Beatrice?"

"It is, but last name is not Hind. My last name is Fore. Agent Fore."

"Bea Fore?" Mrs. Marshall grinned. "I guess it beats Bea Hind."

"In comparison, it kicks butt, doesn't it?" she smiled back.

Finally, they got the right people on the phone. With the information that Mr. Paul was himself locked in the vault and unable to help, and verification from Agent Fore/Hind, Sonya received the emergency code. It took over thirty minutes.

"I bet they are good and toasty in there by now," Agent Fore grinned. "These old vaults don't have fresh air pumped into them. Probably claustrophobic too. That's a lot of people in a small space." She looked at the SWAT members. "Ready, team?" She paused for confirmation. "Unlock it, Mrs. Marshall, then please immediately step aside."

The code released the door, and it slowly opened. Agent Fore laughed at the sight of all the droopy looking elves. Santa had removed his beard and suit, holding it on his lap. Joanelle Peters sat wrinkled looking in the corner, mascara marks streaming down her face. Mr. Paul slept like a baby.

"Arrest them all," she barked. "Except the man in the corner."

"What?" Mrs. Marshall exclaimed. "Seriously? They were held hostage like I was."

"No, they weren't, Sonya," Beatrice told her, pulling her aside. "They wanted to make you think that. But that was only because your husband and kids messed up Joanelle's original plan."

"Joanelle? I don't understand."

"The bank robbers that held you hostage were a ruse. After their clean getaway, she would trigger the alarm or phone the police about the robbery. The police would have put up roadblocks across the city, searching for three robbers. Even if they found the culprits, there was no loot to tie them back to the robbery. She'd sent them out with dummy loot bags filled with your fake presents."

Mrs. Marshall stared in disbelief.

Agent Fore continued. "While we sent our forces chasing the robbers, Santa and his elves would quickly tear down the Christmas event and pack it all up in their truck outside, along with the real loot from the other Santa bags. They'd just drive away with no pursuit. It was a brilliant plan, but we caught the fake robbers leaving, forcing her to play hostage and hope she got away with it."

"Why would she do it? She was already wealthy."

"She wasn't wealthy the way you think. She'd gotten most of her money by swindling the bank, via loans she arranged for imaginary customers. That's where Lucy Doom came into the picture. She had agreed to go along, for a cut of the money. Lucy went on the site visits, but there would be no site to see. The two of them would hang out in some city for a couple of days, then come back saying the company checked out. Lucy began stressing over the thievery, her health beginning to suffer. When Lucy changed her mind about participating any further, and possibly coming clean, Joanelle arranged her accident as a stern warning to keep her mouth shut."

"That's terrible."

"I believe Lucy provided the tip. She gave credible examples to investigate."

"That makes sense."

"Joanelle almost got caught in her first scheme to siphon money from deals when Herman reviewed that big deal. Fortunately for her, he made a mistake while removing her 'fee.' She leveraged his mistake to let the deal die to cover her tracks. Nearly getting caught, she switched to the fake company scheme. It proved much more lucrative and had less scrutiny."

"So why the bank robbery?"

"One last score, I think. Nothing proven yet. We began closing the net around her fake loan scheme. Probably figured she'd get a big score with the robbery and disappear."

At that minute, a SWAT team member came forward, dragging Lindsay by the arm. "We found this young lady hiding under a desk in Mrs. Marshall's office."

"That's my daughter!" Her mother pulled her close for a hug. "I'm so happy you are safe."

"You hid under that desk the entire time?" Agent Hind asked, not believing it.

221

"Yes, sir. Er, ma'am." Lindsay looked at her. "You're a police officer and don't work at the bank?"

"Correct. Agent Fore," she replied, accepting the generalization.

Lindsay giggled.

"Yes, your mother and I have talked through the name thing already." She adjusted her uniform. "I guess hiding under the desk is more believable than some of the other weird stuff I've heard today from your family."

"Ma'am?" the officer SWAT team member inquired.

"Yes?"

"We also found bags of loot in Mr. Wilson's office. Not sure how it got there. Santa over there claims it magically floated there by itself."

"Great," Agent Hind groaned. "They are going to *love* this report at HQ."

Mr. Marshall and Benjay appeared. A round of hugs within the Marshall family ensued. Mrs. Marshall smothered her son with attention, looking at his patched up arm.

"How did you get past the front door into my crime scene?" Beatrice asked.

"We walked in," said Benjay.

"You just walked in the front door?" Agent Fore asked.

"Yes, ma'am, we did."

"I'm going to have to remind some people around here of protocol."

"Did you find out what's in the old wooden boxes?" Benjay asked.

"What boxes?" Beatrice asked.

"The old wooden boxes in the secret passageway," Benjay replied, not in time to see his sister zipping her lips.

Agent Hind sneered at Lindsay. "Hiding under a desk, eh?" She turned back to Benjay.

Lindsay broke her silence. "It's really cool back there. And creepy. I mean that somebody can look into the offices from back there."

"And the boxes are back there?"

"Yes, in a room at the end." Lindsay pointed to the front. "Under the stairs."

"What's in them?"

"We don't know. The door was hard to move. It's dark and scary in that room, with spiders." Lindsay's shoulders shivered.

"Big spiders," Benjay added, cringing.

"Really big spiders," Lindsay emphasized, making her eyes big.

"I get it. Spiders," Beatrice replied.

Benjay spread out his hands. "Really, really big spiders!"

"Show them the way," Agent Fore said, motioning to the SWAT members.

Five minutes later, SWAT team members carried the old wooden boxes out of their hiding spot, placing them on the table in the vault. They pried one open, Agent Fore looking inside.

"Well, I'll be," she said, reaching in, pulling out a gold bar.

"OMG!" screamed Lindsay at the dazzling block. "Is that real gold?"

"I'd say it is."

"I wonder how it got there," Sonya Marshall said.

"I did a lot of research on this bank before taking this assignment," Beatrice replied. "There was an unsolved robbery here over seventy years ago. The police just assumed the robber got away with the gold. It appears they left it and never got back to collect. Looks like I'll close two cases today," she grinned. "Thank you, kids! Not only are you heroes, but you made my day!"

"Can I keep one of the gold bars, since we found them?" Benjay asked.

Everyone laughed but him.

"They are property of the bank," his mother replied. "Maybe Mr. Paul will give you both something as a finder's fee."

"Cool," Benjay replied. "Hope it's enough to get a Super Jet Flying Alien action figure."

Lindsay laughed. "Let's hope so, since I think this Santa won't make any deliveries this year."

"It's okay," Benjay grinned. "I already mailed my list to the real one."

Beatrice looked at Benjay's mother. "You and your family can leave, Sonya. We know where to find you for further statements."

Sonya Marshall smiled, nodding.

"You know where you won't find *me* tomorrow? At the bank working." Beatrice laughed.

On the drive home, they tried to piece together everything that had happened on this crazy, snowy day. They grabbed a few sandwiches off the table in the bank, but they'd gotten soggy on the inside and too crunchy on the outside by then. The Marshalls arrived home, hungry and exhausted from their unplanned excitement. The almost blizzard-like drive didn't help either. Walking into their home, they agreed that after looking at everyone's perspective, everything seemed to fit into place. Except one thing.

"Bubbles!" shouted Benjay.

"Exactly," said Mr. Marshall. "Why did the Bubbles need to protect you?"

"No, I mean the Bubbles are here. Look!"

Mr. Marshall put down his keys, smiling at the floating Bubbles. "Thanks again for all you did today. I am extremely grateful."

"Yes," seconded Mrs. Marshall. "Thank you for keeping Benjay, and Lindsay, safe."

"Which," Mr. Marshall said, "brings me to the thing we can't figure out. Why does my son need protecting by Bubbles?"

"Seer said Benjay is important to our clan's future. Maybe to all Bubbles. It's vital we keep him safe," Peepers blurted out. She covered her mouth after saying what she'd overheard spying on her mother and Fret. She knew she'd be in trouble with the Elders for saying that to the humans. More time added to her off-Globe restrictions, she worried.

227

"We've said too much already," Fret said, frowning at his sister, disappointed that she'd spied on his private conversation with their mother, and more so that she told the humans. "We're just glad we could help. Stay safe."

They began to leave. Peepers turned back.

"It was nice to see you again, Benjay," she smiled, blinking her overly large eyes. "Please stay out of danger." She pouted. "I doubt they'll bring me along next time."

Did you love this novel?

Let the world know!

I appreciate every honest review of my work on Amazon, Goodreads, or your favourite book lover website.

Amazon link:
https://www.amazon.ca/Dale-J-Moore/e/B004F7MBX8

For an Independent author and publisher, this is the best advertising that I can receive.

Thank you,

Dale J. Moore

Didn't Start with Bubbles Book 1?

Bubbles 1: A Story of Wonder

A boy and his family, magical creatures with special abilities, and environmental crooks.

What if your new best friend was a Bubble – one that talked and flew? How would you get anyone, especially your parents, to believe you?

Seven-year-old Benjay Marshall wishes people treated him normally. He feels normal; he's just missing part of his leg after dealing with cancer. Fueled by an overactive imagination and a humourous way of expressing himself, Benjay's life takes an extraordinary turn due to a chance encounter with a magical Bubble. As he learns more about the Bubbles, the more he realizes his family will think he's simply spinning another tall tale.

With his father in grave danger from crooks sabotaging his environmental project, how does Benjay make his family trust that Bubbles are not only real, but are possibly the *only* chance to save the day?

An uplifting children's adventure
Bubbles 1: A Story of Wonder is a page-turner, exhibiting healthy doses of humour, wonder, and mayhem along the way. Sure to be enjoyed by both boys and girls.

Books in Other Genres

Futuristic Thriller

Ubiquitous Medical
We're Everywhere, For You!

Dale J. Moore

UbiquiMed: We're Everywhere, For You!

The world had changed. A violence Plagued nation, torn apart by a financial crisis, struggled to find its way back. Disease and poverty were rampant. Government assistance led to government intervention. Thus emerged Ubiquitous Medical, a federally funded health organization designed to fill every need of a desperate public.

"UBIQUITOUS MEDICAL is a fast paced ride that will keep you guessing. Twists and turns keep you on the edge of your seat, while the characters grow and deepen with every page. Dale J. Moore's voice shines through in this unique tale of a chilling future."
Gemma Halliday, award winning author of the High Heels Mysteries

Trials of Katrina Series

Amateur Sleuth / Romantic Comedy

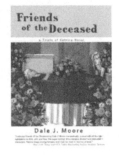

"I enjoyed Friends of the Deceased by Dale J Moore tremendously, a novel with all the right ingredients to thrill, chill, and keep the pages turning! Witty dialogue, likable-- and dislikable!--characters. Katrina keeps moving forward, and I look for more in this line of books."
Heather Graham, New York Times and USA Today Bestselling Author

Check out the FIRST book in the series,

Life of the Party
Maureen P. Moore

'Outgoing? Gorgeous? Enjoy P/T evening work? Good fun! Good pay! THIS IS PERFECTLY LEGAL!' The ad in the Toronto paper sounds just about perfect for Katrina. Except for the 'outgoing' part. Desperate to escape a creepy roommate and a scary landlord, she must find some way to supplement her meager café salary to flee to a new apartment.

Eye-popping beautiful but woefully shy, when Katrina is hired as a professional guest (aka PEST) for a company called Life of the Party, her nerves get the best of her. Before she can make a total fool of herself and lose her new job, she's saved by a dashing and mysterious stranger who vanishes into the night.

With the help of her newfound friend and fellow PEST Cathy, Katrina tries desperately to find her mystery man. Her search, and her life, gets disrupted by the nefarious affairs of her roommates, landlord, and new boss. Along the way, Katrina learns that she may be shy - but she's certainly no wallflower.

The Second book in the series,

Friends of the Deceased
Dale J. Moore

How does a small town girl end up investigating crime at a funeral home in Toronto? Drop-dead gorgeous Katrina is trying to run her new salon and take her relationship to a new level. The unexpected death of a client and struggles with her salon lead her to the Shady Rest funeral home.

As she stumbles her way through the personal problems that plague her world, Katrina ends up immersed in the world of preparing people for the next world. With the help of a ruggedly handsome police detective, some old friends, and a few new ones, will she get to the bottom of what's going on, or end up buried by it? One thing is certain; when Katrina gets involved, chaos and comedy will ensue.

"Friends of the Deceased features Katrina (Kat), a heroine who refuses to be daunted by lies and treachery and finds a silver lining because of her kindness."
Carolyn Hart, Author of the Death on Demand series.

"Behind-the-scenes hijinks at a funeral home will have you cheering for hairdresser Katrina and her gang when they delve into stolen goods, fraud, and charity scams. Katrina has to unravel the mysteries before the next ultra luxury casket is made for her."
Nancy J. Cohen, Author of the Bad Hair Day mystery series

The Third book in the series,
Days of Wine and Tomatoes
Dale J. Moore

Katrina is back for her third chaotic adventure! Trying to revive a struggling relationship with her detective boyfriend, they're off for a long weekend to wine country along the shores of Lake Erie. Customary to Katrina's exploits, trouble crosses her path like a black cat, altering the idyllic getaway.

As the town of Leamington holds its annual Tomato Fest, the summer waterfront party atmosphere is disrupted by a kidnapping. Mixing the enjoyment of the lake front wineries with sleuthing and rooting out clues, Katrina missteps from one mishap to another while solving mysteries in her unique way.

Having been the Life of the Party, and after surviving Friends of the Deceased, Katrina's latest escapade has barrels of wine and laughs. Mix in a bushel of tomatoes, a misfit crew, and the summer sun, and you've got Days of Wine and Tomatoes.

"A rollicking respite perfect for a lazy spring afternoon."
Deborah Coonts, Author of the Lucky O'Toole Las Vegas Adventures

Thriller

If life gave you a death-defying wake-up call, would you sit back counting
your blessings or realize you'd been given a second chance?

Dr. Tre Brightman seems to have it all. A young dentist with a Hollywood clientele and movie star relationships, he's living the high life. A fatal tragedy leaves him seriously injured and drives him to evaluate his actions and the casualties he's left along the side of his road to success. He embarks on a cross-country journey of atonement, unaware that one of those victims is determined to resolve their past conflict – permanently.
Tre's quest devolves into a physical and psychological battle of endurance leaving him to wonder if he'll survive to make Amends.

Made in the USA
Las Vegas, NV
15 November 2023

80876657R00134